POWERS OF OBSERVATION

Powers of Observation is a collection of familiar essays presenting the author's reflections on life, literature, and travel, and thus constituting a 'shadow biography' of George Woodcock.

During his distinguished career as a travel writer, poet, biographer, social historian, and essayist, George Woodcock has published over 50 books, receiving the Governor General's Award for *The Crystal Spirit*, the Molson Prize, and a host of magazine writing awards. His contribution to Canadian culture is immeasurable.

POWERS
of
OBSERVATION

George Woodcock

Quarry Press

The publishers thanks The Canada Council and the Ontario Arts Council for assistance in publishing this book.

Most of the essays collected in this book previously appeared in *City & Country Home* magazine.

CANADIAN CATALOGUING IN PUBLICATION DATA

Woodcock, George, 1912–
Powers of Observation

ISBN 0-919627-15-3

I. Essays. II. Title.

PS8545.O6P69 1989   824'.008   C89-090005-1
PR9199.3.W66P69 1989

Cover art by M. Stewart, from The Canada Council Art Bank. Reproduced with the permission of the artist. Photo documentation by Yvan Boulerice.

Imaging by ECW Production Services, Sydenham, Ontario.
Printed by Hignell Printing Limited, Winnipeg, Manitoba.

Distributed by University of Toronto Press, 5201 Dufferin Street, Downsview, Ontario M3H 5T8.

Published by *Quarry Press, Inc.*, P.O. Box 1061, Kingston, Ontario K7L 4Y5.

CONTENTS

FOREWORD

It would betray the spirit of these essays if I were to write a long and solemn introduction. So this foreward briefly combines acknowledgment with explanation and does very little else.

I have long been interested in the kind of brief literary essay which the French called a *feuilleton* and which the English called a middle, because it appeared customarily as a kind of reflective interlude in a magazine, situated between the main articles and the book reviews. Such pieces combine brevity of form with breadth of reference and speculation as they range without any strict limitation of subject or mood over the whole realm of thought and feeling. One of Aldous Huxley's characters in *Antic Hay* refers to them as "delicious middles," and at their best they sustain the tradition of one of the great English-language genres, that of the occasional essay. Essays of this kind, without a rigidly defined didactic purpose, without the narrowing of focus that is inevitable in reviewing a single book, offer a range of comment and reflection on literature and life that is not easy to any other form.

Lately, with their increasing concentration on events and current issues, periodicals have been less and less inclined to find room for essays of this kind. I had been thinking for some time of a way to revive them when I was approached by Charles Oberdorf, Senior Editor of *City & Country Home*, who invited me to contribute to his magazine a series of short casual essays of the very sort I had been considering. He suggested that a flexible consistency might be established by the essays being based on brief quotations that had special resonance for me. I tried out the idea with a couple of essays — the first in this volume —

which Charles and his associates liked, and my pieces have been appearing in *City & Country Home* ever since March 1985.

There is no arrangement of these essays other than the order of original publication. Nevertheless, I think those who read them with a touch of empathy will become aware of a temperamental consistency, of a steady attitude to life and art, and of a pattern of linked interests. I have been able to write about the books and sometimes the people that have attracted and influenced me, and often of the far travels that have been the other side of my continuing education. And in the process of weaving together all these threads of interest and activity, the informal sketch of a life inevitably appears, and rather more than the sketch of a view of existence. I have not set out to make these essays a kind of shadow autobiography, but recollection appears in many of them, and the personal viewpoint is essential to such writings.

Yet in the process of pursuing personal interests, I have attempted a more disinterested task, that of making my readers aware — or sometimes merely reminding them — of books I have chosen, because discussing them seems to open the mind's eye; I hope that reading these essays will be as pleasing as writing them has been.

Finally, I must thank Charles Oberdorf and the editorial staff of *City & Country Home* for their continued encouragement and their sensitive editing of my essays.

POWERS OF OBSERVATION

Daily it is forced on the mind of the geologists, that nothing, not even the wind that blows, is so unstable as the level of the crust of the earth.

Charles Darwin,
The Voyage of the Beagle

Thus, on his way into the Andes from Valparaíso in March 1835, CharlesDarwin summarized his reactions on finding, at nearly 4300 metres above sea level, beds of fossil remnants of shellfish that once crawled at the bottom "of a moderately deep sea." Many times over I have read *The Voyage of the Beagle*, the account of the long journey on a pre-Victorian survey ship that between 1831 and 1836 took the young Darwin (not quite twenty-three at the beginning of the trip) on a journey around the world that shaped his whole future life. Especially in the Galápagos Islands, with their extraordinary forms of life preserved and perfected over millennia of isolation, it gave him the material for his major work, *The Origin of Species*, in which he propounded the theory of evolution by natural selection that has been the subject of unending controversy ever since the book was originally published in 1859. It was followed in 1871 by Darwin's other epoch-making book, *The Descent of Man*, which exasperated orthodox Victorians and continues to exasperate Christian fundamentalists by declaring that man too — like other living creatures — was not created according to the account in Genesis, but also evolved, presumably from some humbler ape-like kind, by the survival of the fitter members of each generation.

I have never been wholly convinced by Darwin's explanation of evolution. Like George Bernard Shaw and Samuel Butler, I cannot help believing there is more purpose in the way life has developed and diversified than can be explained by mere survival of those who have been fortuitously better equipped.

This does not mean that I accept — except as a wonderful metaphor — that the world and all our ancestors were created, as according to *Genesis*, in seven days. It does mean I see a creative intelligence at work in the universe, and in our own intelligences, by which men and mosquitoes direct their lives and plants direct their growth, as merest sparks from that inexplicable force which has operated over all the eras past time, its beginning unfathomable, its ending unimaginable, its nature probably unknowable. Perhaps this is the Unknown God whose altar St. Paul found in the agora at Athens.

I don't accept everything Darwin said, yet — as I remarked — I return to *The Voyage of the Beagle* because of the special quality of the narrative. Darwin was only one of the great Victorian naturalists who wrote superbly vivid travel books. George Orwell and John Middleton Murry and I shared a special affection for *The Naturalist on the River Amazons* by Darwin's friend, the entomologist H.W. Bates; it is an inimitably intimate account of life on the great jungle river in the 1840s, before the rubber barons moved in and destroyed it. Another marvellous scientist's travel book of the same period is Thomas Belt's *The Naturalist in Nicaragua*. Belt was a geologist, but his great avocation was collecting tropical butterflies and, while hunting specimens as a mining engineer in Nicaragua more than a century ago, he wrote an account of life there which provides excellent background for those interested in a place once very much out of the world's eye but now so often in the news.

What these Victorian writers and others like them share is a vast receptiveness to new experience and minds wide open to the earth over which they travelled. None of them were scientists of a kind all too common today — confined to their specialties and intent on promoting their academic careers. These men went into the world to see it whole, and their eyes were open to a good deal more than the fossils at their feet. On the same day as he observed the seashells at nearly 4300 metres and commented on the unstable levels of the crust of the earth, Darwin ascended through snow to a crest and looked out with joy at the prospect. His description is one of clear concrete images leading up to the final expression of emotion:

> The atmosphere resplendently clear; the sky an intense blue; the profound valleys; the wild broken forms; the heaps of ruins, piled up during the lapse of ages; the bright-coloured rocks, contrasted with the quiet mountains of snow; all these together produced a scene no one could have imagined. Neither plant nor bird, excepting a few condors wheeling around the highest pinnacles, distracted my attention from the inanimate mass. I felt glad that I was alone; it was like watching a thunderstorm, or hearing in full orchestra a chorus of the Messiah.

While it probably isn't true that there's nothing new under the sun, history and even one's own life are full of resonances, and reading Darwin's account of crossing the Andes at 4572 metres I am reminded of crossing the range even higher, at 4780 metres, by the astonishing railway — the highest in the world — built by British engineers between Lima and Huancayo.

We had left behind the green lines of terraces the Incas planted up to 3962 metres, but still, near the very top of the pass, people were living around a copper mine which, in my own Andean travel book, *Incas and Other Men*, I describe as "a jumble of corrugated iron buildings clambering up a cliffside like a Pueblo village and reflected in the mirror of a tiny lake." If I did not see any of Darwin's shellbeds, I did see testimony to human endurance, that of the Indian miners who could work so hard at a spot where I was hit by mountain sickness so that even my speech became disjointed: "like sentences spoke this I," and so on.

But I did, the other day, find a haunting anticipation of Darwin's shells, in a passage by the old Ionian poet-philosopher Xenophanes, who wandered around the Greek settlements in Sicily 2500 years ago. Always seeking evidence about the origin of life, Xenophanes gave what may be the first account of fossil marine life on dry land. He recorded shells found in the mountains, "and in the quarries of Syracuse an impression of a fish and of seaweed has been found . . . and in Malta flat shapes of all marine objects." Xenophanes concluded the earth must once have been covered in mud as a result of being "carried down into the sea" and that the mud preserved the impression, an insight astonishingly close to the conclusions of modern geologists.

And he decided this — at the very beginning of science as an exercise in human reason — without a background of research, without instruments, without anything but keen eyes and an inquiring mind.

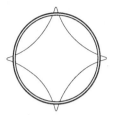

MEDIA AND MESSAGES

Here They Speak and Tell the Story . . .

Aucassin and Nicolette

The medieval romance *Aucassin and Nicolette* was written seven or eight hundred years ago by an author whose name has long been lost and forgotten. A version — the only one known — was found centuries later in an old manuscript now in the Bibliothèque Nationale in Paris. It was published and translated in the nineteenth century, but only when Oscar Wilde's teacher, Walter Pater, the great English stylist, praised it in *Studies in the Nature of the Renaissance* (1873), was it recognized as a charming minor classic, brief and romantic enough — like *The Rubaiyat of Omar Khayyám* — to become a popular Edwardian gift book.

Thus I encountered it, in a copy I still have, given to my mother by my father on the Christmas after my birth: a pretty little volume with limp embossed cover of puce suede, handmade paper inside, and gaudy pictures of hero and heroine. I suppose those bright little pictures first led me to pore over the book, and I probably read the story with the mild contempt with which small boys often regard tales of romantic love. But what soon impressed me was that, unlike any other book I had seen, it was divided into prose and verse. Each passage of verse was preceded by the rubric, *"Here They Sing."* And each passage of prose, in the old Victorian translation, was preceded by another, *"Here They Speak and Tell the Story."*

13

Long before I began to write, the latter phrase set me thinking about writing. I saw in it a distinction between the act of speech and what was said — between, as we would say today, the medium and the message. A glimmering sense of the distinction between form and content began to emerge in my mind.

Years later, when I read the original in Old French, I saw the distinction there was even more elaborate. *Or dient et content et fabloient*; here one speaks and narrates and makes a story. Writing about the time of Richard Coeur de Lion, the author must have meant this as a direction for telling the tale to illiterate audiences (one person singing and the other narrating). To make sure, he brought in even more distinctions than the translator — between speaking and telling and making a *fabliau*, as such tales were called in medieval France.

The English phrase stuck in my mind until all I could remember clearly of *Aucassin and Nicolette* were the words "Here They Speak and Tell the Story." They have preserved me safely from the arguments of people like Marshall McLuhan that "the medium *is* the message." I *know*, stubbornly and from long ago, that the story is more than the speaking.

Aucassin and Nicolette, verse and all, is no longer than many modern short stories: a moving, at times surprisingly ironic, tale of erotic possession. Aucassin, *li biax, li blons, / Li gentix, li amorous* (the handsome and blond, the noble and loving), is a young Provençal nobleman who falls into a love so commanding that he cannot carry out his knightly duties; his father, the Count of Beaucaire, threatens to kill Nicolette, the girl bought from a Saracen slaver and converted to Christianity who has captivated his son. It is *Romeo and Juliet* with a happy ending. There are escapes from high towers, wanderings in forests and far lands, captures by pirates, but in the end all is well; Aucassin finds that his "sweet friend," whom he adored for herself alone, is a real princess, daughter of the "King of Carthage." True love is doubly rewarded.

Simple though it sounds, *Aucassin and Nicolette* is a work of many aspects, romantic but at times realistic to the point of cynicism. The visual descriptiveness is sometimes conventional, as when the narrator describes Nicolette's "laughing blue eyes" and "lips more red than cherry . . . ." But elsewhere he becomes ironically extravagant, clearly mocking romantic convention as when, for example, he tells of a sick man cured by the mere sight of Nicolette's ankles. If *Aucassin and*

Nicolette moves out of its time by its ironic mockery of romance, it does so also by its use of prose to tell a tale.

To us it seems natural that prose, which is nearer than poetry to everyday speech, should be the medium we use most. But that is the reaction of people used to reading and writing. Preliterate people — and perhaps postliterate people will be the same — have a greater respect for the structures of verse, more complex than those of prose. The Homeric epics, the *Iliad* and the *Odyssey*, are very elaborate works, but they were composed by oral bards and spoken from memory by professional reciters or *rhapsodes* before they were put down in writing, somewhere about 550 B.C., at the order of Peisistratus, the remarkable tyrant of Athens, who also patronized the festival of Dionysius, where drama as we know it originated in the Greek tragedies. It was only after people began to read widely that prose appeared in ancient Greece, when, about 2450 years ago, Herodotus wrote his account of the wars of the Greeks and Persians, the world's first great prose work and also its first great history.

Again, in the Dark Ages, after the fall of the Roman Empire, illiteracy became general, and the first writings to emerge were verse, like the Anglo-Saxon epic *Beowulf* and the French *Chanson de Roland*. Once again, prose was a sign of growing literacy; not long after *Aucassin and Nicolette*, still in the twelfth century, Geoffrey of Monmouth wrote his *History of the Kings of Britain* in prose. Prose is more accurate; verse more evocative. *Aucassin and Nicolette* stands between and has some of each.

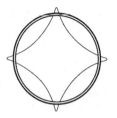

EDITORIAL MEMORY

Sooner or later
it all comes thronging back
everything that ever happened to you . . .

Al Purdy

Somewhere near the end of his twenty-seventh book of poems, *Piling Blood*, Al Purdy is remembering a journey to the Arctic made years before. He sees himself once again standing on the stony shore of an arctic island, watching the icebergs and involuntarily breaking into song. His singing attracts the sled dogs, and they gather round him and howl their lamentations:

> they sang the soul's grief of being trapped
> and knowing it inside an animal's body
> and the dogs mourned

Like many of Purdy's poems it is a bit of experience recalled and put into verse in a way that makes it sound like a universal statement on the condition of living beings. For man and dog are presented as equal in the face of life; a little earlier in "Dog Song 2," as the poem is called, Purdy says of himself that

> you stand on your hind legs and sing
> because you're a dreaming animal
> trapped in a human body

Whatever our species, we are all caught in a mortal frame, and our hunger to transcend it is ironically subject to biological laws we cannot overcome.

It isn't a new thought. In a more famous poem, "Sailing to Byzantium," Yeats talked of the heart being "fastened to a dying animal" and longing to be transformed by "the artifice of eternity." The paradox of consciousness and mortality has puzzled many poets in many times.

But this wasn't all Purdy's poem set me thinking about. Talking of everything that happens to us "thronging back," it also raised the question of the role of memory in literary creation. There is Wordsworth's famous remark about poetry springing from "emotion recollected in tranquility," which sets the memory right at the heart of literary creation. And, indeed, we do write out of the recalling of our experience. Mordecai Richler once remarked that the first twenty years of life should give a writer all the material he will ever need for the rest of his career. But Wordsworth's statement is slyer and more complex than it appears. Poetry is indeed emotion recollected, but recollected in a different situation and mood than that in which it was experienced, and so is changed into something else; it is transformed by memory.

In the long shelf of books that makes him Canada's most prolific poet, Purdy has dealt greatly with the past. He has written splendid poems not only about his own youth but also about the lives of ancestral figures, the Loyalists who first inhabited the rural Ontario with which he is most familiar. Poems like "The Country North of Belleville" are rhapsodic elegies whose evocation of a way of life already past seems to belie Canada's claim to be a new country.

> And where the farms have gone back to forest
>   are only soft outlines
>   shadowy differences —
> Old fences drift vaguely among the trees
>   a pile of moss-covered stones
> gathered for some ghost purpose
> has lost meaning under the meaningless sky
>   — they are like cities under water
> and the undulating green waves of time
>   are laid on them —

If, as Purdy says, "it all comes thronging back," it comes mingled with other memories and changed in the process. A decaying farm is seen resembling a drowned city and so becomes a metaphor for the impermanence of human achievement.

In other words, memory has done something with the straightforward perception of experience, and here we come to the point where human memory will always differ from computer memory. Computer memory records. Human memory incessantly creates. We remember the past as it never was. This was the great truth that Marcel Proust developed in *Remembrance of Things Past*, transforming our conception of the writer's role, and killing the whole realistic idea that literature could portray things as they are or were. Proust taught that as soon as an experience is past, memory begins to modify it, to reshape it to the mind's idea of what is shapely and meaningful. That is why Proust warned us against going back to places that glow in our memories. We shall be disappointed, not because the places have changed, but because memory has changed them for us. What we remember is not what we once experienced.

It is perhaps the most important realization of modern literature. It has released writers — and readers — from the demands of plausibility. Since memory is an act of the imagination as much as an act of recording, we are, therefore, free to accept any mixture of fiction and fact. Once one admits the creative role of memory, one's view changes, even of kinds of writing that claim to be chronicles of actual happenings. How "true," in the sense of describing things as they happened, is autobiography? If the autobiographer has any scrap of literary feeling, it is manifestly not "true," partly because material has to be selected to save the reader from being swamped in the flood of tiny facts and episodes that make up every day of our lives, partly because we all create myths about ourselves and shape our recollections to fit, and partly because a book, if it is to have any appeal to the reader, has to have a form which restricts its contents. The famous "candid" *Confessions* of Jean-Jacques Rousseau were in fact a clever portrait of the author as he wished to be seen.

This may suggest that an autobiography is inevitably an act of deliberate invention. But that isn't really so. The memory does its shaping before the writer ever gets down to work, and his material is already pre-selected and arranged before he puts his fingers on the keyboard.

So, ultimately, I really disagree with Purdy's statement that "everything that ever happened to you" comes "thronging back." Only as much as the memory chooses comes back. And that is why the workings of memory — its powers of creation and limitation — have become so important to modern writers.

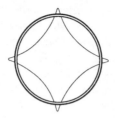

POWER AND COMPASSION

True human goodness, in all its purity and freedom, can come to the fore only when its recipient has no power. Mankind's true moral test, its fundamental test (which lies deeply buried from view), consists in its attitude towards those who are at its mercy: animals.

Milan Kundera,
The Unbearable Lightness of Being

Those words were not written by a North American animal rights activist but by the Czech novelist Milan Kundera, who was one of the leaders of the Czech revival of the 1960s, when the New Wave in film emerged largely through his influence, and when Alexander Dubcek tried to liberalize the régime. In 1968, the Russian army invaded Prague and the "human face" that Dubcek had tried to give to socialism was brutally torn away like a mask. Kundera was one of the first to suffer. He was dismissed from his university post. His books were removed from the shelves of libraries. In 1975, in despair, he finally left his country, and in 1979 his Czech citizenship was taken away.

Kundera's most recent novels are about his country under the post-1968 Russian domination. *The Farewell Party, The Book of Laughter and Forgetting, The Unbearable Lightness of Being*: are all about tyranny and its effects, mainly its moral effects. For what Kundera is really telling us is how a totalitarian régime, where the secret police are everywhere and everyone can be a secret policeman, will rot the very fabric of society, which is trustfulness. Kundera doesn't have the apocalyptic streak that George Orwell developed in *Nineteen Eighty-Four*. He doesn't show us a society where terror reaches into every corner and the citizen's movements are completely controlled by it. Where people find themselves trapped in intolerable situations, it is often because they have not been wary enough. But wariness has its price, and the real subject of Kundera's novels is the way that lying to the state leads men and women to lie in their relations with each other. Because the totalitarian state has destroyed the kind of natural trust and cooperation that should exist in a free society, infidelity flourishes, and Kundera's novels are inhabited by petty Casanovas seeking freedom through promiscuity. They are guilty, they feel compassion for their victims, but they find it hard to stop.

And here we come back to the matter of animal rights, and the quotation I used at the beginning, to which I would now like to add another. It is from the Vancouver *Sun* account of a hearing of the Royal Commission on Seals and Sealing. A sealer is defending killing seal pups. Seeking some kind of comparison to justify himself, he says: "You can take for instance a hangman. He's got a job." With a different intent, the sealer is doing just what Kundera does: equating brutality between men with brutality between men and animals.

Kundera is really telling us that when the state becomes so powerful that trustfulness between human beings is destroyed, then men and women become ruthless towards each other. The relations between human beings become similar to the relations between humans and animals because, in such circumstances, humans, like animals, have no power.

Human relations with animals are central to *The Unbearable Lightness of Being*. Tomas, the leading character, is a brilliant surgeon driven out of his profession for a single indiscreet statement; eventually he becomes a window cleaner, which gives him ample scope for philandering, while his companion, Tereza, serves in a bar. Tereza's sense of being the victim of Tomas's infidelities becomes unendurable when she finds a crow that has been maltreated by boys. The dying crow seems to symbolize her own situation, and she persuades Tomas to leave the city. He becomes a driver in a farm collective, so humble that at last, even if he has lost everything except the love of the woman to whom he was perpetually unfaithful, he is at least not persecuted. Once he has nothing to lose except his life, the state leaves him alone.

But now the relationship between men and animals takes another turn. The last days of Tomas and Tereza, before they die in a car crash, are centred on their feelings for the dog Karenin, their last link with the city world. Karenin's devotion, Tereza's love for him, Tomas's compassion as Karenin dies of cancer, unite them in a haunting bond, until Tomas gives Karenin the injection that puts him out of pain. A lesser writer might have made that ending sentimental. But Kundera concentrates the novel's whole meaning into this final scene.

Basically, Kundera tells us what the ecologists and the environmentalists have been teaching, that every form of life is biologically linked to every other, and any disturbance of the balance will lead to unpredictable and probably disastrous consequences. Kundera sees a moral ecology in which cruelty towards powerless beings — men or animals — affects all of society. As William Blake wrote: "A dog starved at his master's gate / Predicts the ruin of the State."

Perhaps history proves them both right. Cultures that encourage cruelty to animals encourage cruelty to human beings as well. Spain, where bullfights flourish, was the scene of one of the most brutal civil wars of history. In early nineteenth-century Britain, when such atrocious spectacles as dogfights, cockfights, and bearbaiting flourished, men and women were hanged for stealing out of hunger. And so Canadian issues like the seal hunt not only reflect our relations with animals; they also concern our relations among ourselves.

THE BREEZE FROM THE EAST

When he asked her to marry him, the wall at the end of the alley fell down and a breeze stole in from the Far East, with a vision of palms and pomegranates. She accepted him for the sake of her imagination.

Sara Jeannette Duncan,
His Honour, and a Lady

There is a quick flash of self-revelation when Sara Jeannette Duncan — in my opinion one of Canada's best and least recognized novelists — relates the lines above about Judith Church, the heroine of her novel of British India, *His Honour, and a Lady*. By marrying the right man, Judith is elevated from the fate of an old maid in a grey English industrial town to become a *burra memsahib* at the height of the Raj. There is also a typical Duncan irony, dry and sharp, in the second sentence. Judith marries to escape into the bright light and broad horizons of a distant land. Yet having committed herself to dull John Church, who eventually becomes acting lieutenant governor of Bengal, she respects the devotion and idealism that make him a fine administrator, and when she does fall in love with one of his colleagues, she refuses to yield to her emotions, sustaining her loyalty to the man she does not love but admires.

Duncan is drawing an interesting distinction here between various human drives, specifically between imagination, which is a matter of the mind, and love, or passion, which is a matter of the feelings. In

Judith Church, imagination is stronger than passion. This goes against the accepted canons of romantic fiction, but it fits the ambivalences of Duncan's own career as the emancipated young Canadian woman who became the dutiful Anglo-Indian wife and indeed wrote a novel entitled *The Simple Adventures of a Memsahib*.

Like all novelists, Sara Jeannette Duncan wrote out of experience, even when her fiction was not autobiographical in the strict sense. And dutiful Judith Church is a reflection of one facet of her character. To Canadians, Duncan is best known for *The Imperialist*, her novel about Canadian political life in a small town — in my view the best Canadian novel up to the time Morley Callaghan wrote *They Shall Inherit the Earth* in the 1930s. But most of Duncan's writing life was spent in India, and at least half her fiction is based on her very shrewd perceptions of the British ruling class there.

She made a career in her early twenties as one of the first women journalists in Canada, and it was a world tour to gather material for articles in the Montreal *Star* that first took her to India in 1889, when it seemed as if British rule would never end. The pomp and glamour of the Raj stirred the imagination of the girl from Brantford, Ontario. In Calcutta, which was then the imperial capital, she met a gentle young English museum curator, Charles Everard Cotes, and on a moonlit evening at the Taj Mahal she let her irony slip for a while and accepted his proposal in that classically romantic setting. Being at heart a very conventional woman, Sara kept her faith, and during the long years of her life in India was never one of those weaker memsahibs whose temptations and occasional lapses from grace she describes with such strange sympathy in books like her recently reprinted volume of short stories, *The Pool in the Desert*. Yet, as we reluctantly gather from *Redney*, Marian Fowler's biography of Sara Duncan, it was less an enduring love than a Presbyterian sense of duty that kept Sara with Everard.

It was something more that made her persist so long in the puzzling, often painful love-hate relationship with India which so many of us share. I have been travelling to India and back for more than twenty years, almost as long as Duncan's on-and-off residence there, and as I read her books on the country (not only her novels and stories but also her marvellous memoir, *On the Other Side of the Latch*, about all she saw and thought in a summer convalescing from tuberculosis in a chaise longue on a Simla lawn) I recognize the ebb and flow of feeling India creates among those who become entrapped by its ambiguous and complex charm. One starts with a somewhat innocent wonder at all the strange variety of the land and its life; I find that wonder when I dip back into my own first book on the country, *Faces of India*, as I do when I read Sara Duncan's first enthusiastic essays from 1889. The latest of my Indian books is called *Walls of India*, and the difference between *Walls* (which suggests irrevocable divisions) and *Faces* (which suggests openness to the world) is the measure of my changed mood. I left for the last time two years ago so exasperated with the problems of Indian travel that I felt I would never return, but I know now that I shall not be able to keep away. The charm is working again. Sara Duncan must have experienced the same conflict, for she often felt the desperate need to leave India, but kept returning for a quarter of a century.

These ambivalent feelings towards India, which so many people experience, are not merely individual. The recent rise of British nostalgia for the days of the Raj shows a similar sea change of feeling among a whole people. In 1947 the British, by and large, were glad to get rid of the responsibility of India, and though a few novelists like John Masters (*Nightrunners of Bengal*) pegged away at novels about British India, there was no broad revival of interest in the country until the late 1960s. Then *The Jewel in the Crown* and the other books in Paul Scott's *Raj Quartet* began to appear, arousing interest in a country that had by then become unfamiliar to most younger English people. Scott's novels had a double-sided appeal as they told the story of the bonds and the hostilities that the long years of the Raj had created between the British and the Indians; the whole sad tale was far enough away to seem suddenly exotic, yet near enough for many people in Britain to remember as part of their own lives. After *The Raj Quartet*, a flood of popular romances about the Raj began to appear, and then came the films *Gandhi* and *A Passage to India*, and the television dramatizations of Paul Scott's novels, all of them massive and misleading in their achievement, since they were trying to do something as difficult and frustrating as fixing for permanent record the colour of a chameleon.

India defies the simplicities that are necessary for stage and screen.

The written word, which leaves room for hesitancies and qualifications and the variations of tone needed to re-create such a complex country in the mind, has always been more faithful. E.M. Forster's novel *A Passage to India* was far more true to the life he saw and shared than the film that bears its name. Here in Canada, if we are going to make a cult of reviving India's past, there is a great justification for reprinting Sara Duncan's Indian novels. For in novels like *His Honour, and a Lady* and *Burnt Offering*, this Canadian writer rendered with impeccable subtlety both the glamour and the tedium of the Raj. Perhaps she did so because she became so dedicated to her writing that her personal relations grew remote; Marian Fowler, in *Redney*, quotes a suggestive and revealing remark Duncan once made to an interviewer: "One sees oneself projected like a shadow against the strenuous mass of the real people, a shadow with a pair of eyes."

What strange and touching and disturbing things that pair of eyes saw, and with what luminous imagination the writer — like her heroine Judith Church — presented them!

WORDS OF LOVE

Few people would fall in love had they never heard of love.

Duc de la Rochefoucauld,
Maxims

Recently I have been reading two weighty works on love. One is a reprint of Denis de Rougemont's *Love in the Western World*, which was first published almost half a century ago. The other is a massive three-volume book called *The Nature of Love* by Irving Singer, which has recently been printed. Denis de Rougemont works on a rather narrow canvas, talking about the concepts of love that appeared among the French poets of the middle ages, concepts that have given us the idea that love and passion are somehow identical. Irving Singer's book is much more ambitious, a great panoramic survey of ideas about love from the ancient Greeks down to the present. All kinds of love come under his intense scrutiny, including the love of God as well as love between human beings.

One thing that struck me, reading these two books together, was that both of them brought in that seventeenth-century French wit, the Duc de la Rochefoucauld, and quoted the same maxim: "Few people would fall in love had they never heard of love." La Rochefoucauld spent his life coining such phrases, which he collected in a book called *Maxims* that had a great vogue in eighteenth-century France as a kind of cynic's handbook to life. He had the same kind of ability as Oscar Wilde to cram a great many implications into a single witty saying, and indeed some of his maxims read as if Wilde had originated them. "Hypocrisy is the homage that vice pays to virtue." "We all have strength enough to endure the misfortunes of others." La Rochefoucauld turned out such pithy aphorisms by the hundred, and in all there lurks a barbed truth, so that one very often has the feeling that he was not really a cynic at all, just more honest than most men care to be.

In their various ways, I think both de Rougemont and Singer agree with La Rochefoucauld. De Rougemont's theme is that the lovers in most poems and novels are not really in love with human beings but with the idea of love. Passionate love of the kind immortalized by Antony and Cleopatra he regards as a harmful concept invented by the troubadours in the twelfth century. It blinds people to human values and has led generations away from a balanced view of married love. Instead, couples idealize love in a defiance of the world that leads to self-destruction, like the love-death (*liebestod*) that Wagner celebrated in *Tristan und Isolde*, where the pair of star-crossed lovers find fulfilment only in death. Singer is rather less sensational than de Rougemont, but even he, as he works his way through the philosophers, poets, and novelists of the past, is forced to the conclusion that our views of love are shaped by what is written about love.

We live in a world awash with words about love, in print and in films, in pop music and classical opera alike. None of us escapes these words, and thus there are fashions in love just as in clothes, fashions that depend largely on the way love is talked or written about at various periods. In ancient Athens heterosexual love was undervalued, and the ideal love was between men of like minds. The troubadours despised married love; to them the true lover adored someone else's wife but never hoped to sleep with her, which would have been breaking the rules of the game. In classic nineteenth-century novels, from *Tess of the d'Urbervilles* to *Anna Karenina*, love always ended tragically. In twentieth-century Harlequin romances it always ends happily.

Some novelists have written about people destroyed by words of love. Flaubert's Madame Bovary and Thomas Hardy's Eustacia Vye in *The Return of the Native* are both hollow women whose minds are so filled with ideas about love absorbed from romantic literature that they embark on adventures that can only bring them to messy ends. And which of us, if we are honest with ourselves, will not admit to having at some time thought of love as it is depicted in novels or on the screen, as something that happens to Richard Burton and Elizabeth Taylor and can happen that way to all of us? Who has not, in youth, felt like the young man on his first date in a poem from Glen Sorestad's *Hold the Rain in Your Hands*:

> Trying to recall
> what all those paperback lovers said
> failing to remember

Apart from the basic factor of sexual desire, are words all there is to love? Let's look again at La Rochefoucauld. He doesn't talk about "loving" but about "falling in love." And he has another neat saying: "The mind is always the dupe of the heart." Perhaps the real difference is between "loving," which is something that we do in full consciousness, and "falling in love," which is a matter of the feelings, or to use the poetic language, "of the heart." After all, as another great phrasemaker, Blaise Pascal, once told us: "The heart has its reasons which reason knows nothing of." I am irresistibly tempted to enter the aphoristic competition and end with a phrase of my own: True love lies deeper than words.

FOR TRAVEL'S SAKE

For my part, I travel not to go anywhere, but to go. I travel for travel's sake. The great affair is to move.

Robert Louis Stevenson,
Travels with a Donkey

I was brought up with the puritanical idea that one did nothing in life for the sake of doing it, but with a Purpose, an End in View, whether it was to make a fortune or enter the Kingdom of Heaven. It was the same with travel. One travelled to the nearest town to shop there, to London to work there, and even on holiday the destination was the important thing, the beach at Blackpool or Brighton where one set about enjoying oneself, since this was what one had come for. The journey — the way between departure point and destination — was a necessary operation but of no significance and to be completed with seemly rapidity: no idle lingering by the way.

By the time I read Stevenson's *Travels with a Donkey* I was as familiar as most boys then were with *Treasure Island*, but that I regarded as fantasy and not real life. *Travels with a Donkey*, an account of Stevenson's wanderings with a rather diminutive pack animal through the Cévennes, a mountainous region of southern France, was very much real life. And as I read, I found myself beginning to absorb the spirit of Stevenson's talk about going and moving and *travelling for travel's sake*. For Stevenson in *Travels with a Donkey* had no real destination at all. He entered a region that was historically interesting and visually striking, and he wandered there, accepting the chances of each

30

day's travel, the little adventures, the human encounters, and weaving them not into a tale with a beginning and an end, but into a kind of picture of an unfamiliar country.

In *Travels with a Donkey* and his other books about directionless travelling, like *An Inland Voyage* and *In the South Seas*, Stevenson was one of the influences that turned me, in time, into a travel writer. And once, at least, I paid my tribute by adopting his title, *In the South Seas*, for a series of films I wrote for the CBC about the various Pacific island groups. On that journey, I remember well, I had to be grateful to Stevenson for more than inspiration. Two places where our paths crossed, with an interval of eight decades, were the Gilbert Islands — where Stevenson lived for a while on an island called Abemama, the Place of Moonlight — and Samoa, where he lived out his last six years and died in 1894.

The Gilberts are the quintessential coral islands, atolls of reefs and palm-groved islets surrounding vast lagoons, with never for thousands of square miles a place in sight much more than five feet above sea level. Their haunting atmosphere is perhaps most thoroughly evoked not by Stevenson, but by a former British colonial officer named Arthur Grimble, who lived there many years and wrote a couple of books — *A Pattern of Islands* and *Return to the Islands* — about the exiguous existence which the Gilbertese eked out, dependent on the scanty resources of sea and coral strand and haunted by an often hostile spirit world. (Even in 1972 I was warned never to speak to a strange man walking north; he might be a dead man making his way to the local Hades at the top end of the chain of atolls.)

Grimble, I found, was better remembered than Stevenson in the Gilberts. He was tall, very thin and taciturn; one day an old Gilbertese said to me: "We would be sitting in a room and it would be as if the ghost of a reed had entered silently." In that image there was a great deal of the Gilbertese obsession with the spirit world, the world of walking dead, for the "ghost of a reed" was in real life a practical and sound administrator.

Samoa was the place where Stevenson was remembered. The Samoans are Polynesians, much concerned with rank and prestige, and in some way Stevenson convinced them that he had both, so that he was revered as the *Tusitala*, or Teller of Tales; his mountaintop tomb

31

on the island of Upolu is still a place of pilgrimage, and the big house he built at Vailima is now the king's residence.

We benefited from Stevenson's prestige when we wanted to go to Apolima, the smallest of the Samoan islands. The people there are so conservative that we had to go accompanied by a nobleman, with whom we set out, from the lagoon of Upolu and out over the stretch of open sea towards Apolima, in an old, rickety whaleboat run by an outboard engine. On the way our guide and sponsor remarked that it might be a good thing if we could offer some titles. My wife had baronial links in Austria; there was no difficulty with her. What could I offer? I was a mere writer, I remarked. His face lightened. "Perfect," he said. "Ever since Stevenson, *Tusitala* is an honoured title here. That is how I shall introduce you — the Teller of Tales!"

And so he did. With hearts in our mouths, we endured the shooting of the dangerous L-shaped passage into the lagoon, an intricate matter of judging the right wave and the crew fending off rocks with poles as the boat surged at full speed on its devious way into the calm water beyond. The chiefs were coming down the beach to greet us. Presenting our ritual gifts of canned corned beef (called *pisupo* in Samoa because the first cans to arrive there were of pea soup) and Australian silver dollars, we sat down in the *fale* (the open-sided meeting house) to a traditional feast. Our noble friend introduced us; the chiefs grunted in satisfaction each time the word *Tusitala* came up, and I gave silent thanks to Stevenson's ghost. Everything went so well, indeed, that the chiefs proposed to elect me an honorary *matai* — the title of a minor chief who heads a Samoan clan. I had been warned already of the obligations such a title might incur: endless requests to help my fellow clansmen of Apolima. So I remembered Stevenson's dictum that the "great affair" of travel "is to move," and I politely declined a destination among the lesser nobility of Samoa.

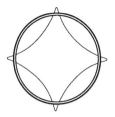

ALICE IN LAMALAND

"Then you should say what you mean," the March Hare went on.

"I do," Alice hastily replied; "at least — at least I mean what I say — that's the same thing, you know."

Lewis Carroll,
Alice's Adventures in Wonderland

When I was a small boy and was told that Lewis Carroll wrote *Alice's Adventures in Wonderland* and *Through the Looking-Glass* for young girls to read, I thought what strange children they must be. For I, simple-minded young male that I was, liked to read either straight and somewhat patriotic adventure, which Henty provided in plenty (*Under Drake's Flag, With Clive in India*, and so on), or stories of human ingenuity, like *The Coral Island* and *The Swiss Family Robinson* and *Robinson Crusoe*, the father of them all, in which people suddenly cut off from the normal amenities made do with splendid self-sufficiency. Carroll's books, with their strange mixture of logical games and parodies and sheer nonsense, in action and in words, exasperated me. Like many children I wanted everything to be straightforward and regarded adult ways, with their endless shades of meaning and nuances of behaviour, as impossibly devious.

Then, as I grew into adolescence, and that priggish little devotee of action dissolved into the aspirant poet, I suddenly found Carroll immensely appealing for the mocking skill with which he would toss accepted ideas about, and the almost glossolaliac inventiveness with which he would play with the language.

> 'Twas brillig, and the slithy toves
> Did gyre and gimble in the wabe:
> All mimsy were the borogroves
> And the mome raths outgrabe.

If Carroll had never written *Through the Looking-Glass*, I wonder if James Joyce would ever have put together that extraordinary mosaic of fractured language, *Finnegans Wake*.

When I read Lewis Carroll talking about meaning in the way he does in the passage quoted at the start of this piece, it seems to me there is a good deal more than meets the eye in his juxtaposition of saying what you mean and meaning what you say. Are they really so completely "the same thing" as Alice claims? Saying what you mean is a problem of the exactitude of language. Meaning what you say has another dimension, to do with the integrity of thought. *Alice's Adventures in Wonderland* is full of sententious little remarks of this kind which, taken in context, mean more — or even something else — than what they say. "Take care of the sense, and the sounds will take care of themselves," for example, was on one level a parody of the arguments of certain late Victorian poets that the sound of a poem was important and the sense did not really matter. But forget about the parody and apply the saying to a piece of Carroll's like "Twas brillig . . . ." At first it seems nothing but sound — strange sound. But gradually a kind of meaning comes out of it. On one level Carroll was, of course, parodying once again, here the kind of verse that was just a collection of poetic clichés. Take a poem beginning, say, with the words:

> 'Twas even, and the jocund birds . . .

replace them with:

> 'Twas brillig, and the slithy toves . . .

and you find the poem makes almost as much sense and the sound pattern is if anything more interesting. But once you have read the poem often enough an odd kind of meaning seems to emerge out of the nonsense, and we end with a strange obscure vision of weird creatures writhing in a primaeval marsh.

I have always thought that Lewis Carroll's sense of the instability of meaning was due to his being a mathematician and therefore accustomed to a spectrum of meaning different from the one provided by language. I have had no reason to change that view. But another assumption I held about Carroll for a long time — that his plays on meaning would be difficult for a non-anglophone to understand — proved on one occasion at least to be entirely unfounded. And thereby hangs a tale.

One day in 1970 my wife and I set off from Dehra Dun in northern India to see a Tibetan potentate, the Sakya Lama, who had established himself with a thousand followers in a bit of jungle at the foot of the Himalayas. There was no road in; we had to travel by jeep, with two Buddhist nuns as fellow passengers, along narrow jungle paths where the branches lashed our faces and for five kilometres over a dried and stony riverbed where the going got so rocky that the nuns were sick and continued to vomit and pray until we finally reached the old zamindar's grange where the Sakya Lama lived. He came out to meet us, a figure out of the Tibetan middle ages: a tall and portly man clad in a gown of gold brocade, his hair coiled in plaits above his round face and secured by a jewel of ruby and gold, big turquoise rings hanging from his long, distended earlobes.

We immediately started in to dispatch the contents of an immense table, slurping our noodles loudly in accordance with Tibetan etiquette, eating our way through piles of pork and chicken, dumplings and vegetables, while the Sakya Lama told us of his role and rank. Head of the oldest Tibetan Buddhist sect, the Sakyas, he was not a monk like our friend the Dalai Lama. He was a layman, a kind of sacred king revered for the traditions he embodied. He had even, he said rather ruefully, to marry shortly in order to ensure the hereditary succession of the Sakyas. We then talked a little about the needs of his settlement, with which we were able eventually to help through the Tibetan Refugee Aid Society in Vancouver, and then I complimented him on the excellent English he had acquired since he fled from Tibet in 1959.

He brightened greatly at this. He enjoyed English, he said. He enjoyed reading English books. What books did he particularly like? I asked. "*Alice in Wonderland*," he answered, and for the moment it seemed hilariously incongruous, to be sitting here in sight of the snow peaks of the Himalayas, talking with this man who seemed to have stepped out of a distant Central Asian past about the March Hare and the Mad Hatter.

But there was an odd rightness to the situation, as there is to much about Lewis Carroll. Tibetan Buddhists are great logic choppers; in their monasteries they used to hold endless debates on shades of meaning, and the Sakya Lama loved that side of *Alice in Wonderland* — the more paradoxical the better. I asked him about the nonsense verses. No problem there, he assured me; they had their own mantras which the monks chanted, and these were so old that nobody really understood their meaning, but perhaps for that reason everyone believed they were very potent. But best of all, he said, with a great smile irradiating his round face, framed by its huge earrings, he liked the Cheshire Cat; it was such a splendid image for the Buddhist belief in the transitory, illusory nature of the physical world.

That night, up in the old hill station of Mussoorie, where we slept, I dreamt of the Sakya Lama, and his smiling face became transformed into that of the Cheshire Cat. As in the book, "It vanished quite slowly . . . ending with the grin, which remained some time after the rest of it had gone."

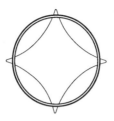

HOW TO BECOME
A GENTLEMAN

*I am fond of digging in the garden and I am parshial to ladies if they
are nice I suppose it is my nature. I am not quite a gentleman but
you would hardly notice it but cant be helped anyhow . . . Your
old and valud friend*

ALFRED SALTEENA

Daisy Ashford,
The Young Visiters

There have been some strange best-sellers in the history of the popular
novel, but none, I think, as strange as *The Young Visiters*. It was
published on May 22, 1919, and before the end of the month it had
been reprinted twice. There were no fewer than five reprintings in June,
and at least four more in July. My copy belongs to the fourth July impression, the twelfth printing of the book in just over two months. How
many further impressions followed in that distant year of 1919 I do not
know, but I do know that the book has been reprinted at steady
intervals over the intervening decades; less than a year ago I saw a new
edition. *The Young Visiters* has obviously been in print for most of the
sixty-seven years since it first appeared, and I suspect every copy
published has been read several times; certainly my own has not suffered from neglect.

The most extraordinary thing about *The Young Visiters*, in view of its
great and sustained popularity, is that it was written at the end of the

nineteenth century by a girl of nine, Daisy Ashford. Daisy's photograph is the frontispiece to my copy of the book; she is a plump child with a knowing smirk, dressed in one of those sailor suits adapted to the female figure that the Victorians loved. Daisy wrote her novel in a twopenny notebook, stealing time on wet days; the first page of the original manuscript is also reproduced and shows Daisy to have been less than a copperplate prizewinner. The story lay forgotten until, more than 20 years later, it came to the attention of J.M. Barrie, the creator of *Peter Pan*, and with his introduction it found its path to immortality.

The Young Visiters is really a story of social pretensions, a theme much favoured by the British but rarely shown from the standpoint of the nursery. Following standard romantic procedures, Daisy arranged her characters and their actions into a novel variant of the eternal triangle.

The story opens with Alfred Salteena, a casualty of the Victorian social system; his mother was a Miss Hyssopps of the Glen, but his father was merely "a first rate butcher," so that he is not quite a gentleman but hopes one day to become "the real thing." Mr. Salteena, "an elderly man of 42" (but not impervious to romance) is fond of asking "peaple" to stay with him, and as the novel begins his guest is "a young girl . . . of 17 named Ethel Monticue." (To the knowing young Daisy this household situation does not seem in the least curious.) One morning there arrives "a quear shape parcel it was a hat box tied down very tight and a letter stuffed between the string." The box contains "the most splendid top hat of a lovly rich tone rarther like grapes with a ribbon round compleat," and the letter is from a real gentleman named Bernard Clark, inviting Mr. Salteena to visit him and "bring one of your young ladies whichever is the prettiest in the face." So the two set off, Mr. Salteena not eating an egg for breakfast "in case he should be sick on the journey," and Ethel applying "some red ruge . . . because I am very pale owing to the drains in this house."

Mr. Salteena takes Bernard into his confidence about his social ambitions, and Bernard sends him to the Earl of Clincham in the Crystal Palace, who undertakes to turn him into a gentleman for £42. The high point of his education is a "levie" at which the Prince of Wales (later Edward VII) is seated on a golden chair "in a lovely ermine cloak and a small but costly crown." Later, the Prince confesses his weariness with court life. "It upsets me said the prince lapping up his strawberry ice all

I want is peace and quiut and a little fun and here I am tied down to this life he said taking off his crown being royal has many painfull drawbacks."

While Mr. Salteena has been mingling with princes and prime ministers and admirals, all enthusiastic consumers of ices as they talk "passionately about the laws in a low undertone," Ethel has stayed with Bernard, who has fallen in love with her and spirited her away to the Gaierty Hotel in London. During a boat trip on the Thames he proposes to her: "taking the bull by both horns he kissed her violently on her dainty face. My bride to be he murmured several times." They are married in Westminster Abbey, to Mr. Salteena's great chagrin: "he ground his teeth as Ethel came marching up." But eventually, all ends well for everyone. Working fast, Ethel and Bernard return home from their six weeks' honeymoon in Egypt "with a son and hair a nice fat baby called Ignatius Bernard." And Mr. Salteena gains acceptance in Court circles and "managed to get the job his soul craved and any day might be seen in Hyde Park or Pickadilly galloping madly after the Royal Carrage in a smart suit of green velvit with knickerbockers compleat."

The Young Visiters was Daisy Ashford's only novel, a solitary masterpiece. (Her short stories, published in 1920 in *Daisy Ashford: Her Book*, were not nearly as popular.) The mystery remains why *The Young Visiters* was so successful. As a tale it is admittedly no more ridiculous than the average Harlequin romance, but that is not enough to explain such great and immediate acclaim. The secret, I suggest, lies in the time of its appearance. A few people were probably delighted merely by its special mixture of precocity and innocence, but more, I think, recognized it as an unconscious mockery of the pretensions of gentility that had flourished in the Victorian age, and that by 1919 had become thoroughly discredited. In the world where Aldous Huxley wrote his satirical novels and Lytton Strachey debunked the Victorian age in his notorious biography of the great queen herself, the desire to be a gentleman began to look absurd.

In this situation, *The Young Visiters* had an effect similar to the exclamation of the child in Hans Christian Andersen's story: "But the Emperor has nothing on at all!" In her own way, as innocently but as tellingly as Andersen's child, Daisy Ashford, who listened so carefully to what her elders said and did not always get it right, was exposing the whole world of absurd conventions by which the Victorians lived. Mr. Salteena chasing in his velvet suit after the Royal Carrage became as potent an image as Andersen's naked emperor. "Out of the mouths of babes . . . ."

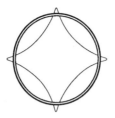

LIVING IN THE IMMATERIAL WORLD

In theory one is aware that the earth revolves, but in practice one does not perceive it; the ground upon which one treads seems not to move, and one can live undisturbed. So it is with Time in one's life.

Marcel Proust,
Within a Budding Grove

Marcel Proust wrote one of the world's great novels, in size as well as in importance. The French edition of *Remembrance of Things Past* which I brought back from Paris 30 years ago runs to 15 buff-coloured paperback volumes and occupies just over two feet of my bookshelves. Rich as it is in dramatic human encounters and bizarre characterizations, *Remembrance* centres primarily on the ambiguous relations between time and memory and on the way in which memory, which is a subjective function, conditions our ideas of time.

In the process Proust casts doubts on the whole realm of our perceptions of reality and on their relation to what is actually there. We perceive the revolving of the earth, he suggests, only in a curiously inverse way, because to us it seems that the sun is revolving around a static earth. When we get up each morning, we still witness something very like what the ancients perceived as the sun-god Helios driving his fiery chariot up into the heavens each dawn. But our conflicts between perception and reality go much further than our observations of daily phenomena. They condition and have always conditioned the relationship between common sense and science.

In the eighteenth century there was an Anglo-Irish bishop named George Berkeley who argued that matter has no real existence. It appears to exist only because it is perceived by the eyes of men or the mind of God. That very down-to-earth man, Dr. Samuel Johnson, was highly disturbed by such a proposition, particularly as his disciple, James Boswell, presumed to remark that it was impossible to refute Berkeley's argument. "Striking his foot with mighty force against a large stone, till he rebounded from it, Johnson roared, 'I refute it *thus*.' "

Common sense had spoken, even at the expense of a set of sore toes. But science throughout the ages has nibbled away at such assumptions of a sound and solid world. Long ago, when Buddha was alive, in the sixth century B.C., the Indian philosophers along the Ganges had already evolved the first atomic theory. They had no scientific equipment — only their reasoning powers — but they had realized that matter is never stable; metals rust, stone wears away, water vaporizes, all forms dissolve with the passage of time. They proposed, therefore, an ultimate minuscule entity, the atom, of which all things are composed in various combinations. But nobody ever saw an atom. Reality had now retreated beyond the bounds of perception.

Later on, in the service of science, technology extended the limits of perception; with microscopes and telescopes we saw more minutely and more extensively. But still the ultimate reality of matter remained elusive, until in the end Bishop Berkeley seemed to have the laugh over Dr. Johnson. Matter as actual substance, the scientists finally concluded, did not exist. Even the atoms, which the ancient Indians and Greeks had thought of as the ultimate particles, had no existence as solid entities. They were charges of energy, full of destructive power but perceptible only in their effects. The desk at which I write, the page on which you read this essay, are in the eyes of science "such stuff as dreams are made of," immaterial forces that have assumed transient form. All this we have come to know and believe, and Dr. Johnson would be quickly laughed out of court if he came back with his stone and his scuffed shoe to battle for the solid and objective reality of matter.

And yet, as Proust argued, we perceive and act in contradiction to what we know. Our time zones are based on the assumption of the sun moving round the earth rather than of the earth revolving; we get up "when the sun rises" and we take our evening drink "when the sun is over the yardarm," in contradiction to all astronomical truths. We have enough practical knowledge of what happens when we journey around the earth to deride those who still claim the globe to be flat, but in practice, when we plan our roads and cities, we accept a pattern of straight lines which assumes the earth *is* flat. It is only when we plan long air journeys that we accept Einstein's insight that the shortest distance between two points is not necessarily a straight line.

We live double lives, in fact, one life according to science, which teaches that nothing exists as we see it, and the other according to our daily experience and perceptions, in which desks are solid wood and toes still hurt when they kick stones, in which the sun rises daily and the flowers bloom and the birds sing. And we rejoice in our delusions.

THE SPLITTING IMAGE

*It is the common wonder of all men, how among so many faces,
there should be none alike.*

Sir Thomas Browne,
Religio Medici

My father was an impoverished bibliophile — none poorer in the dark days of the Depression — but he was also an astute philatelist, and on the rare occasions when he ran across a Cape Triangular or a West Australian black swan and sold it advantageously, he would invest the profits in original or facsimile editions of minor Elizabethan or Jacobean classics. And so, at a comparatively early age, I was dipping into such exotic writings as Thomas Nashe's *Pierce Penniless His Supplication to the Devil* and William Lithgow's *The Total Discourse of Rare Adventures and Painful Peregrinations* (complete with graphic pictures of his tortures during the Spanish Inquisition), and peeking secretly at Sir Thomas Urquhart's racily bawdy translation of François Rabelais.

Somewhere on the more serious side were the works of Sir Thomas Browne, one of the most learned and self-effacing men of the seventeenth century. Browne was probably the best-trained doctor in the England of his time. He graduated from Oxford and then travelled across Europe to attend the great medical schools of Montpellier in France, Padua in Italy, and Leyden in the Netherlands. But, instead of gaining a fortune as a physician to the rich in London, Browne retired to the small town of Norwich in East Anglia, where famous people

44

travelled to visit him, and he wrote a series of books reflecting on the destiny of man. These were so clearly argued that even as a boy I found sentences that leapt at me from the page, irradiated by their obvious truth.

One of them told me: "No man can justly censure or condemn another, because indeed no man truly knows another." I was so impressed by that thought that I repeated it to my father the next time my mother prodded him into standing judgment on my actions. His answer, as I remember it, was that Sir Thomas was a philosopher who was thinking in terms of high principles, while he and I were debating petty crimes. But I still remained impressed with Sir Thomas's dictum, and even more with the aphorism quoted at the beginning of this piece, though a haunting question about that one remains.

"It is the common wonder of all men, how among so many faces, there should be none alike." I am sure Sir Thomas was right. I have never in my longish life seen anyone who was the true spitting image of myself or of anyone else I know, and I challenge my readers to examine their memories and decide whether — individually — any of them has ever met his or her true double. I know that there are "lookalikes" who at a short distance may appear the real thing, but that is a different matter.

When Prince Charles married Lady Diana, a competition was arranged to find the new princess's double. Hundreds of rivals came forward, and one was finally picked as the nearest. In some ways the resemblance was astounding. Eyes, hair, and complexion were the same, the shapes of nose and chin exactly corresponded, and a clever hairdresser had worked wonders. Yet it remained a striking resemblance; nothing more. The two young women looked alike but not identical, and the real difference, I think, lay in the mind. For it is the mind — and all minds are certainly different — that gives the face its range of expressions, and it is the expressions playing across it over the years, rather than mere physical characteristics, that in the end give a face its true individuality.

But even if it is doubtful whether or not real doubles exist, the idea of the double fascinates human beings. Literature is full of them, from Dickens to Conrad, from Dostoyevski to Stevenson, and they offer a favorite theme for theatre and cinema. The reason, I suggest, is that most of us feel both divided and incomplete. Somerset Maugham expressed the feeling well in *A Writer's Notebook*, a quotation that in its own way balances the one with which I began.

> There are times when I look over the various parts of my character with perplexity. I recognize that I am made up of several persons and that the person which at the moment has the upper hand will inevitably give place to another. But which is the real me? All of them or none?

Writers, and artists in general, are especially prone to feel that they are possessed of multiple personalities. They often talk of having a writing persona who is different from their everyday persona. (The very word *persona* is significant: originally it meant the mask a Greek actor put on when he assumed the character of Oedipus or Orestes in one of the great plays of Sophocles or Aeschylus.) Very often the play of masks will go so far in a writer that he not only assumes a different name, like Samuel Clemens writing as Mark Twain, but also allows the persona with the *nom-de-plume* to take over his life. This certainly happened with George Orwell, who in the end was known under his real name of Eric Blair only to his bank manager, his parents and siblings, and his very early friends. For later friends the mask of the writer had completely hidden the ordinary man; we talked to him as George and many of us did not even know that he was also Eric.

The idea of presenting a series of masks raises the question whether our personalities are just a series of surface effects, as some Buddhists believe, or whether there is someone real and hidden who wears all these masks turn by turn — a real *self*. I think the uneasiness among many people regarding their overt personalities, and the consequent search for a real self, has also had something to do with the strength of the idea of a double. In part that idea reflects the feeling that we are divided beings, but it also reflects the sense that somewhere deep within, or even outside us, is the true self we will recognize and whose appearance will make us whole: the double. The double never does come to complete us, and so we remain what we are, divided, imperfect, incomplete.

But, of course, for the ancient Chinese masters of the art of pottery an imperfection was necessary in a great work of art to preserve it from the perfection of beauty, which is stillness and death. In the same way, as human beings we remain alive precisely because of our sense of incompleteness, because of our longing for that elusive real self to make us whole.

Let me offer a blessing. May you never meet your double!

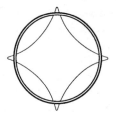

THE HIGH PYRENEES

I'm tired of Love:
I'm still more tired of Rhyme.
But Money gives me pleasure all the time.

Hilaire Belloc,
Epigrams

Because of a single poem, "Tarantella," I have always thought of the high Pyrenees as Hilaire Belloc country. "Do you remember an Inn, Miranda?" he began, and went on:

Do you remember an Inn?
And the tedding and the spreading
Of the straw for a bedding,
And the fleas that tease in the High Pyrenees . . .

But now, for reasons I'll come to, I think the tiny Belloc poem I quote above is more appropriate.

When I first went into the Pyrenees in the 1950s, I actually endured fewer fleas than I had battled in some of the cheap little Left Bank hotels in Paris that my poverty then forced me to share with tarts and students — the whole cast of *La Bohème*, I would sometimes think — without, of course, the voices!

But I do remember the inns of the Pyrenees. Stark stone buildings up narrow valleys with small windows to keep out the cold, and perpetually damp beds and Basque *patronnes* who would always say, when one arrived in the middle of the day, that there was nothing in the kitchen for lunch, and then produce an aromatic herb-filled peasant soup, an omelette with morels, trout freshly caught in the stream and served with delicious tiny potatoes, and a last course of crisp pears and mountain cheese or a crêpe one's palate would long remember.

The Pyrenees were also for me Andorra, that remote little land high in the mountain ridges between Spain and France that, like other such sovereign fragments as San Marino, Monaco, and Liechtenstein, has survived and prospered in a century of big and bellicose powers with only a few square kilometres of land and a few thousand people and no means of defence except tradition. Until a generation ago, Andorra had remained a little realm of cowherds and smugglers, linked by rough mountain tracks with the rest of the world. If the fleas teased anywhere in the high Pyrenees, it had to be there.

But when I first reached the mini-country over a quarter of a century ago, it was just beginning to change. We drove in, I remember, from the old French medieval city of Carcassonne, going through the desolate valleys of Corbières, with the ruined troubadour castles on their hilltops, and at a little spa called Ax-les-Thermes beginning to climb the steep switchback road to the high passes. Long before the Andorran border the road's paving had become rough gravel and a deep fog had descended, through which we crawled past a deserted frontier post. Then, as we reached the height of land and the road began to dip down, the mist suddenly cleared, and Andorra lay below us, its golden castle-dotted meadows dropping into the broad valley, with rocky crags and dark pine woods and little hamlets of grim fieldstone houses.

It seemed, sure enough, the austere mountain republic of one's imagination — until one reached the floor of the valley. There, incongruously, in the towns of Les Escaldes and Andora la Vella, the fever of tourism was beginning to take. The first ski slopes had been made on the meadows, and beside the road, among the old stone buildings, the first hotels had gone up. Their porters, in gaudy uniforms, were standing out on the road, frantically gesticulating at the few cars coming over from France. We found, indeed, a flealess bed in a room still damp from drying plaster. The hotels and their employees seemed as yet intruders in a peasant world smelling of dung, where cows were herded past the hotel doors and a young man's great ambition, as in generations past, was to earn himself a name as a daring smuggler.

I went back to Andorra last fall, and it was then I decided that my first quotation from Hilaire Belloc might be more appropriate to the high Pyrenees than the famous invocation to flea-bitten Miranda. For if any people have been transformed by the pleasure of money, it is the Andorrans.

The mountain mist was still there going up from Ax-les-Thermes, and once again the sun broke through as we tipped over the pass into Andorra. But we were now driving on a broad new highway, and what we saw in the valley below was not the scattered pattern of stone-build hamlets, but a kind of ribbon town of new hotels and banks and stores running down all the way into Andorra la Vella. There were so many cars with Andorran plates that it was hard to park anywhere. The last flea must have fled long ago to join a travelling circus. As for the sons of the smugglers, they were no longer playing dangerous hide-and-seek with the French frontier guards. They were sitting in their big duty-free shops, leaving to their customers the problem of getting the booty over the border. I could imagine them singing . . . not quite Hilaire Belloc's couplet, but something like it. For example:

> I'm tired of smuggling and of arduous crime
> Now easy money flows here all the time.

Is there *no place* where rustic independence and hardy virtue still survive, I asked myself as we checked into a hotel so international — and so efficient and comfortable — that it might have been in Monte Carlo or Los Angeles. And a Mephistophelian echo answered: "No place!"

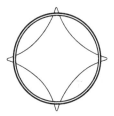

MATTERS OF PREFERENCE

Why have such scores of lovely, gifted girls
Married impossible men?
Simple self-sacrifice may be ruled out,
And missionary endeavour, nine times out of ten.

Robert Graves,
"A Slice of Wedding Cake"

"It was Christmas day in New Delhi," to adapt a famous rhyme, and the local inhabitants, who love junkets of all kinds, were celebrating one of the great festivals of the British Raj with as much zest as they devote to occasions of their own, like the beautiful Diwali, Feast of Lights. I was at a party in one of the large houses near the Lodi Gardens. There was a great central fireplace and the flames glittered on the gold-threaded saris and elaborate heirloom jewellery of the women guests, and on the natty tropical suits and highnecked Nehru jackets of their menfolk. There were high civil servants and rich entrepreneurs, journalists and diplomats — in fact a fair cross section of the new ruling class that in India replaced the British — the class which the Indian novelist Mulk Raj Anand once called "the Brown Sahibs," so completely have they appropriated the fruits of power.

One of the foreign guests was the Mexican poet Octavio Paz, who was then his country's ambassador to India, and he and I stood leaning against the wall, talking literary shop. But our eyes were flitting appreciatively over the room, and Paz finally interrupted our talk of Neruda to sigh and remark, "How marvellous the women are!" And then, with all the eloquence of a Latin shrug, "But the men . . .!" I agreed with a silent nod, and we parted to converse with those fine-looking, self-confident, and splendidly dressed women whose presence in cities like Delhi and Bombay seems to belie the notion of their sex in India as humble and diffident and downtrodden.

I have never quite forgotten the incident, because it represented an attitude I find common among men, though it was quite a long time afterwards that I came across the poem by Robert Graves quoted at the beginning of this essay. Not only poets think in this way. Most modern men do, I suspect, even if they may not always admit it.

But why? Is it a kind of jealousy? When, as often happened, I saw a good-looking and very bright woman student passing out of my university class to devote herself not to a brilliant career but to marrying a young man I found a slovenly bore, did I really want to take his place? I doubt it. I think my reaction was based on much broader feelings than the directly personal one. Graves probably expressed it as well as one can in the last verse of his poem:

Has God's supply of tolerable husbands
Fallen, in fact, so low?
Or do I always over-value woman
At the expense of man?
Do I?
It might be so.

It might be; it probably is. Human beings have a natural tendency to disparage members of their own group, from a small one like the family or the village to a large one like the sex. Nobody is for long a hero to his brother. Most men, if they are not misogynists or so insecure that they fear feminine as they fear other competition, feel more warmly and admiringly towards women than they do towards members of their own sex. The same, with the proper reversals, is true of women.

And this, it seems to me, is the universe unfolding as it should, the proper functioning of yin and yang or whatever name one chooses to give the natural play of feeling between the sexes. Societies like Victorian England or modern-day Indian or Iranian villages, where women are suppressed and hidden and under-valued, are the unnatural ones, just as a society of Amazons suppressing the men would be. The natural society is one where the sexes cherish and admire each other, where men appreciate women for their intelligence, charm, and capability, and women appreciate men for whatever qualities they may mysteriously find in them.

I am aware that here I tread on tremulous ground, for there is no knowing what suspicions may be aroused in the hearts of militant feminists — or of grand misogynists like John Knox with his "Monstrous Regiment of Women" — by such talk of mutual cherishing. I once wrote of a late-eighteenth-century actress, Claire Lacombe, who played an interesting minor role in the French Revolution, and I referred to her as a "beautiful and talented actress." Very shortly I received an angry letter from an English feminist, calling me to order because "beautiful" was a "sexist" word. Would I talk of a "beautiful and talented actor"?

I was at first taken aback by the thought that "beautiful" might be regarded as a sexist word. Is it sexist to talk of a beautiful sunset? Or the beauty of a Mozart aria or of Keats's "Ode to a Nightingale?" Yet I had to admit that I would probably write of a "handsome" rather than a "beautiful actor." And, of course, in the sense of using different adjectives to describe the physical comeliness of women and men, one is giving a sexual connotation to the words. If one talks of a "beautiful man," it is taken to mean that he is more than a little effeminate; to talk of a "handsome woman" suggests that there is a touch of masculine strength in her looks.

But differentiating the sexes does not mean disparaging either of them. It means that, however much we may fight for the equality of rights and opportunities, we cannot avoid some essential differences between the sexes, and we miss a great deal of the wonder and satisfaction of life if we try. Sure, one rarely talks of a beautiful man, but then one doesn't talk of a fatherly woman. "Beautiful" and "handsome" define different kinds of good looks just as motherhood and fatherhood define different kinds of biological and social functions. And in a world where all should be equal and yet are irrevocably different, it is surely a good thing if one side of the equation admires rather than despises the other. And so, like Robert Graves, I find it both wise and pleasant to overvalue women at the expense of men. Wise women, I am sure, reciprocate.

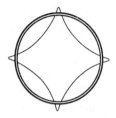

RUNNING OUT OF TIME

And where the farms have gone back to forest
are only soft outlines
shadowy differences —

. . .

they are like cities under water
and the undulating green waves of time
are laid on them—

Al Purdy,
"The Country North of Belleville"

We still often think of Canada as a new country, bounding with youth. The myth of the ever-moving frontier, the ever-waiting wilderness, dies hard. And we forget how in many ways ours is in fact an old country, older than most member states of the United Nations, older even than some of the major European countries: Italy was really united only in 1870, three years after our own Confederation, when Victor Emanuel's troops took Rome, and it was four years after our first Dominion Day that German unity came about in the aftermath of the Franco-Prussian War.

But I don't think it's that kind of political history Al Purdy is talking about in poems like "The Country North of Belleville." What he offers to our imaginations is the rapidity with which in the New World, as our ancestors used to call it, ways of life flourish and decay; towns and settlements and even individual homes and farmsteads go through the same rapid cycle. He is explaining why, in modern Canadian poetry, and Canadian fiction also, there is such a prevalent nostalgia, such a deep sense of departed presences. We have gone through a strange transformation in our consciousness as Canadians. In living memory there was the age of pioneers and settlers, when all our efforts were directed to felling the forest, ploughing the prairie, opening the land to seed and sunlight. Everything was new and vigorous, and it seemed our pasts were somewhere over a great ocean. We did not even think of having histories, let alone writing them. Then we had little literature and less art, for the kind of imagination that produces both lives in a continuum of space and time; we had a great sense of space but almost none of time.

All that has changed. We have our literature and our arts, and both are bound up with the fact that in a generation or so we have acquired a past that is no longer there but here, a sense of history and of living with it. Reading our poets, one is aware of the accelerating process of obsolescence that has overtaken the New World and made it more conscious of its age than the Old.

Compare, for example, the kind of travels one makes on the two continents. In Europe I am always aware of change and continuity coexisting. Old towns have been modernized, but they still stand on their ancient sites, and the centuries mingle in the very fabric of their buildings, the twists of their streets, where life has continued, unbroken by war and catastrophe over the generations. I drive through the French or Austrian countryside. The farm houses may have been rebuilt, but they stand on the same spots as their predecessors. The methods of farming may have changed, and tractors plough the fields instead of horses, but the boundaries have not changed, the deer have been sneaking out of the same wood edges for centuries to nibble the sprouting grain, and generations of peasant sons have inherited the land ever since the Thirty Years War. One is never conscious of decay, of the interruption of life, but always of a living continuity. Everything is in constant use and constant renewal.

But when I go on a journey in Canada, I soon hear the words of the old hymn echoing in my mind: "Change and decay in all around I see." In the cities, buildings barely a quarter of a century old are being bashed down to make way for their successors; older buildings win survival only after desperate heritage campaigns, and then are preserved in tourist quarters like Gastown in Vancouver or Bastion Square in Victoria that mark them off from the general stream of urban life in which a good brick building thirty years old is regarded as too ancient to live. I set out on the road, and all along the way I drive through towns whose centres are dying as trade leaches out to the plazas, or through little prairie communities, like those described in the fiction of W.O. Mitchell and Sinclair Ross, which are now dying because the Trans-Canada Highway has passed them by.

I tell myself at this point that decay is not quite the same thing as history, but when I do seek history in the Canadian landscape, I find it in some self-conscious reconstruction like Upper Canada Village, where people in fancy dress re-enact a way of life dead this century or more. Or I seek it out in one of the ghost towns of the West, which are surely the very symbols of the discontinuity in our history, representing surges of activity that came when some precious metal was found and flowed on to somewhere else when the streams were panned out or the lodes exhausted.

When I am not in such places, which memorialize the decay of ways of life, I am likely to find myself travelling roads where men and women once came and cleared the marginal lands. Now, as in Purdy's poem, the old log buildings are falling down and the bush is creeping around them and an unkempt lilac or an old apple tree bearing small sour fruit is all that is left of the effort to cultivate the land. At such times I have a sense of the age of the land, and it is a melancholy feeling, unlike what I have in Europe, because it is the sense of a lost past that fills my mind, not of a past that continues and flows into the present.

My own explanation for this sense of old age in a new country is that, though we have now acquired a sense of time and are conscious of having a history, we have not yet reconciled it to our expansive sense of space. We still believe there is always room to move on. So the hearts of towns are left to decay while life flows to the suburbs, and the marginal lands are abandoned. Europeans cannot do this; they live out their time within their space, and so there is continuity. We escape into our space, abandoning the present to the past. And that, it seems to the poets, is a way of running out of time.

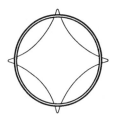

BAUDELAIRE'S
BLUE TROUSERS

Day had fallen and I saw a really fine sight, the sunset; that reddish colour formed a remarkable contrast with the mountains which were as blue as the deepest pair of trousers. After I'd put on my little silk bonnet, I stretched out in the back of the coach and it seemed to me that travelling all the time would be a marvellous life for me.

Charles Baudelaire, 1832

I have always believed that if one looks carefully at what writers and artists do and say when they are children, one can find clues that prefigure their later years. Poets may not be born poets, but the tendencies that incline them to a creative career appear very early and do not need a psychologist to detect them. The two sentences with which I began, by a great French poet, actually come from a letter Baudelaire wrote when he was a boy not yet eleven, attending the hated boarding school to which his military stepfather, General Aupick, had consigned him.

There is still a touch of playfulness, even of naïveté, in these boyish letters of the man who would shock a French nineteenth-century public with the frankness and the literary audacity of *Les Fleurs du Mal*, who emerged as a pioneer in psychedelic lore with *Les Paradis Artificiels*, who acted as spokesman and inspirer of such countercultural trends of the times as Dandyism and Decadence, and who must probably be regarded as the most important ancestor of literary modernism. Yet in these early letters we can also see clearly how he went from there to there, how the child was father to the man and the man to the movement.

Take that first sentence, about mountains and blue trousers, and see it against the background of the 1830s in France. In 1830 Victor Hugo's play *Hernani* had turned the Comédie Française into a battleground between Classicists and Romantics because Hugo had presumed to use some of the language of everyday life. Yet here, only two years later, in the provincial backwater of Lyons, a boy of ten was making a statement even more startling in literary terms than anything in *Hernani* because he was getting his effect by the bold use of incongruity. To compare the mountains with a pair of blue trousers! How outrageous it must have seemed to Baudelaire's solemn older stepbrother when he received the letter! How felicitous it seems to us now! But only because we have the history of modernism between us and the precocious young Charles Baudelaire.

Essentially what Baudelaire was doing in this phrase was what he continued to do in his adult poetry: to seek correspondences, as he called them, rather than similes, which meant recognizing that things were often more strikingly united by unlikeliness than by likeness. This recognition of the mysterious congruity of incongruities became the very basis of literary modernism.

Take one of the most famous modernist metaphors, in the opening lines of T.S. Eliot's *Love Song of J. Alfred Prufrock*:

Let us go then, you and I,
When the evening is spread out against the sky
Like a patient etherised upon a table . . .

Perhaps it's become somewhat hackneyed by now, but I remember reading that passage in the 1920s — as a boy not much older than the Baudelaire who wrote the letter — and being taken aback by the audacity of the juxtaposition of a summer evening and a hospital ward, and yet feeling that I was on to something new and exciting in poetry. Exciting it certainly was, but not so new, for Baudelaire and the French symbolist poets lay behind it, and really it was no more audacious than that boyish comparison of a line of mountains with a pair of deep blue trousers.

The rest of the quotation arouses in me a rather more melancholy reaction. For the boy who put on his little silk bonnet and thought of the wonders of a life of travelling was to become in manhood a restless Ishmael figure who never settled anywhere for long, and who was perpetually starting journeys of the mind that he never completed.

Rosemary Lloyd's collection of Baudelaire's correspondence, *Selected Letters of Charles Baudelaire: The Conquest of Solitude* (University of Chicago Press, 1986), is as sad a book as I have read in a long time. Here are no inspiring dialogues on the art of poetry! The prime subject is money, as it so often is in writers' letters, but exacerbated in Baudelaire's case by the fact that his unimaginative stepfather, General Aupick, locked up in a trust the fortune his real father had left him so that he was unable to pay his debts, and his travelling often consisted of being on the run from his creditors. Difficulties with publishers are — again as with many other writers — the subject of second importance, accentuated in Baudelaire's case by the fact that he tended to write books that angered the censors. The third great subject is sickness; he suffered intermittently the effects of syphilis caught in his youth; it killed him in the end, at the age of forty-six. After all these miseries, Baudelaire sometimes finds the time to say a little about his writing.

And yet, he was writing to his loved and hated mother in 1861, six years before his death, "As I have a cast of mind that is not popular, I won't earn much money, but I'll leave behind a very famous name." And so he did, for in spite of all his troubles and his long periods of chronic idleness, Baudelaire still wrote enough for us to recognize him as one of the great French poets and as the pioneer of modern criticism.

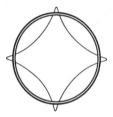

WHOM THE GODS LOVE

Golden lads and girls all must,
As chimney-sweepers, come to dust.

William Shakespeare,
Cymbeline

I have always felt that bittersweet couplet from one of Shakespeare's more melancholy romantic comedies must be read in the same breath as Menander's "Whom the gods love dies young." For when we think of "golden lads and girls" as something more than sunburnt anatomies, it is evident that these are precisely those whom the gods love. Their talent flares early and they seem to shine, when one is in their company, with a lambency that never continues beyond youth.

I have known at least two such people in my life, both poets, whose very faces gave off the light and passion of their poems, so that often the poem and the person reading it seemed expressions of each other. One of them died early, and when I read the poems he wrote in his and my youth, I still see in my mind's eye that golden being and seem to hear the passion in his voice and know for certain that if the gods exist they must have loved him. The other was probably the better poet, but he survived to become a grey, vain old man who wrote no more good verse. Even when I now read the poems of his youth, this living ghost interposes itself, and I realize that here was a golden lad who came to dust merely by surviving; clearly he was one the gods did not love.

Comparing these two poets who were my friends, I realize that in one case the man outlived the poet, whose work was really complete by the time he was thirty. And this leads me to wonder whether the other, the poet who died young, had not also completed his work when the gods abducted him. And this in turn suggests to me that perhaps a person marked from youth to be an artist is never taken away from us before he has completed his work.

Enough well known writers and other artists died young for us to consider the matter in another way. We think of Byron, and his contemporaries Keats and Shelley, dying young of fever and tuberculosis and drowning; of Aubrey Beardsley and D.H. Lawrence, George Orwell and Katherine Mansfield, all dying young of that once romantic sickness, consumption; of van Gogh shooting himself in madness and Pushkin shot in a duel; of Dylan Thomas and Theodore Roethke resolutely drinking their ways to death; and of our own Canadian poets, Archibald Lampman, dead at thirty-eight, and Emile Nelligan, that golden lad par excellence, who started on his career at fifteen, wrote splendidly for five years, and then, at nineteen, retreated into the living death of a madness from which he never emerged, though he lived to be more than sixty.

When I look at these writers and artists, there seems a completeness about their achievement which suggests that if they had lived they would probably have done nothing more of significance. Dylan Thomas's final gallop to death was almost a surrender to the knowledge that he had already ceased to write good poetry. D.H. Lawrence's writing was declining into such absurdities as *The Plumed Serpent* a good five years before he died. Orwell's *1984* had all the ominous finality of a last work. Aubrey Beardsley had ceased to limn the decadent drawings that made him famous even before his final illness set in. Byron's departure to fight in Greece (where he died in his bed) was already a sign that he intended to pass from writing into action.

What fascinates me about many of these writers is that they themselves expressed the feeling of finality. Keats wrote his own epitaph: "Here lies one whose name was writ in water," which is inscribed on his monument in the Protestant cemetery in Rome. Emile Nelligan's most famous and foreboding poem, "Le Vaisseau d'or," ends with lines that seem to anticipate his fate.

Qu'est devenu mon coeur, navire déserté?
Hélas! Il a sombré dans l'abîme du Rêve!

(What has become of my heart, abandoned ship?
Alas, it has foundered in the abyss of dreams.)

Perhaps the most curious instance of this sense of finality is provided in a story Edward John Trelawny told of Shelley. Byron and Shelley were competing as boatmen when the latter revealed to Trelawny that he could not swim. Trelawny offered to give him a lesson, and Shelley took off his clothes and plunged immediately to the bottom of the pool; there he lay immobile, and Trelawny had to rescue him. Shelley commented, somewhat ambivalently, "I always find the bottom of the well, and they say Truth lies there. In another minute I should have found it, and you would have found an empty shell. It is an easy way of getting rid of the body." Only weeks later Shelley was to die by drowning, boating off Lerici.

A final and rather different instance is that of the young French poet Arthur Rimbaud. Like Nelligan, Rimbaud was a golden lad par excellence; he began his poetic career when he was about fifteen and ended it spectacularly with "Une Saison enfer" (A Season in Hell) when he was less than twenty; then he abandoned poetry altogether, his message told. He did not immediately die, or go mad like Nelligan, yet he also underwent a surrogate death, becoming a solitary wanderer, trading and gunrunning in Africa and dying painfully in his thirties, completely indifferent to the fame that the poems of his youth had meanwhile acquired. It was as if another man, a lost golden lad, had written them. The gods evidently did not love Rimbaud as much as they loved the others.

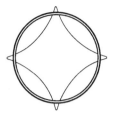

FRIENDSHIPS AND MEMORIES

*As we went out he stepped across the room and gripped my hand
very hard. Queer, the affection you can feel for a stranger . . . I
hoped he liked me as well as I liked him. But I also knew that to
retain my first impression of him I must not see him again; and
needless to say, I never did see him again.*

George Orwell,
Homage to Catalonia

If *Homage to Catalonia* made the same deep and lasting impression on
you as it did on me, you will remember that on the first page Orwell
tells how, when he went to the Lenin Barracks in Barcelona to enlist
and fight in the Spanish Civil War, he had a fleeting encounter with
an Italian refugee. They exchanged only a few words, shook hands, yet,
Orwell felt, "It was as though his spirit and mine had momentarily
succeeded in bridging the gulf of language and tradition and meeting
in utter intimacy." Later on, Orwell remembered that particular meeting and wrote his only good poem about it. It ended:

But the thing that I saw in your face
  No power can disinherit:
  No bomb that ever burst
  Shatters the crystal spirit.

I used the last words of that poem as the title for my own book on

Orwell, *The Crystal Spirit*, because I believed they applied as much to Orwell as they did to that wandering Italian.

I doubt if I would be writing like this if it had not been for an extraordinary happening this very morning. For the past couple of months I have been assembling material for a film that a British-Spanish consortium is preparing on Orwell's time in Spain and the years immediately after. One of the militiamen who served with Orwell on the Aragon front was a dogmatic Trotskyist to whom he referred as "the young American." Yesterday I was looking into the dramatic incident that ended Orwell's career as a warrior, when he was shot in the throat in the trenches outside Huesca. The "young American" had been present, and I turned to an account he had given of the incident — how he had thought Orwell was dying, had cradled his head on his own arm, and later helped to load him onto a donkey to be taken to the field hospital. The young American's name, I found, was Harry Milton. He had been alive four years ago, but whether he still was or where he lived I had no idea. I had never met or been in correspondence with him.

This morning at ten o'clock the telephone rang. It was a strong American voice that first identified me, and then said, "My name is Harry Milton. I was with Orwell in Spain." I said, "The young American!" And he laughed. He had read my book, *The Crystal Spirit*, the previous week, and had rung me up on impulse. We talked for half an hour, Harry retelling his tale, adding details, and then he offered to hand over to me all his records to use as I saw fit. I was grateful for that, but I was even more astonished at the conjunction of events. It was, I suppose, what is usually called coincidence, but I have a feeling it fits in more closely with what Jung called "synchronicity," the meaningful patterning of events that occur in striking conjunction.

It took me back again to *Homage* and the opening page and started me reflecting on the way people move in and out of one's life and what memory does to those relationships. Undoubtedly Orwell was right when he insisted that the vividness of some of the most important encounters one has depends on their brevity.

I think people who travel a great deal often experience such instant and intense relationships. I can remember once, in a forlorn little hotel in the Andes, meeting a young Peruvian engineer so congenial that my wife and I happily travelled with him for three days. We came from entirely different backgrounds, but our minds seemed to open wide to each other. We talked incessantly, and at the end, as we parted on the shores of Lake Titicaca, we swore eternal friendship. Yet we never wrote to each other, never saw each other again, and in that I think we were wise, for I remembered him, and I like to think he remembered me, framed in the totally exceptional circumstances in which we had met. And the result is that to this day — thirty years after — I recollect him very clearly, his looks, his mental alertness, his odd Victorian English, the laugh with which he would correct my dreadful Spanish, his intense hatred of priests, and the way he would bang down the leather cup and shout when we were playing the Peruvian dice game called Dudo. I remember him with warmth and momentary intensity. And I can think immediately of perhaps a dozen intense relationships of this kind, on a ship going down the Red Sea, on an atoll in the Gilberts, at a mission in the Arctic, on a vanished Atlantic liner, framed in time and space and preserved in the memory with all the pristine joy that comes from recognizing a fellow spirit.

I compare them with those other relationships lying dimly in the past, that began with common interests, lasted for a long period and then slowly burnt out, and are remembered far less vividly than the sharp intense travel encounters. After a while one had discovered everything that was interesting about the other people, and then there seemed no point in the relationship continuing, so that by mutual consent it ended, without malice, without regret, and remains like a fading odour in the memory. There is probably something in the Roman adage that familiarity breeds contempt, though perhaps one should rather say indifference. Certainly it is true that those intense brief friendships of travel are rapid explorations of the *unfamiliar*. But what, then, does one make of those relationships that go on for year after year, weathering storms of anger, bridging absences, often joining people of unlike opinions and backgrounds and temperaments, sometimes seeming to sink away like an underground river, then surging up again as strongly as ever and in the mind surviving death?

These, of course are the true friendships, meetings of minds and natures that continue independent of external circumstance, whereas the other relationships I have been talking of are bound by place or time, by a road one travels or a time in one's life. The wonder in the pattern of life is how the long threads of friendship sustain the fabric of memory in which the lost brief encounters still shimmer like vivid strands.

THE NEED FOR ANCESTORS

On the first day of winter
a lonely Polish ancestor
moves in me: she puts on her fur hat
and squints into the sun.

Dale Zieroth,
When the Stones Fly Up

I was thinking about ancestries as I read Dale Zieroth's book of poems, *When the Stones Fly Up*, since I had just finished *Beyond Forget* by Mark Abley, whose articles and reviews in *Saturday Night*, *Maclean's*, and the *Times Literary Supplement* I have long admired. *Beyond Forget* has nothing to do with loss of memory; its title is the name of a tiny prairie community, the focus of the reflective travels that the book describes.

Both Abley and Zieroth spent childhoods in the prairies, Abley moving there with his English immigrant family when he was six, Zieroth descending from European immigrants who came in the great waves of new Canadians ushered in by Clifford Sifton late in the nineteenth century. Read together, their books set me thinking about the special kind of historical vision that prairie people have, and also about the meaning that ancestry holds for us.

Until recently the prairie was no place for rearing poets. It produced realistic novelists like Martha Ostenso and Frederick Philip Grove who presented a dark view of pioneer life. But during the past decade or so some very interesting poets have emerged there from Eli Mandel and John Newlove down to younger writers like Andrew Suknaski and Dale

Zieroth. What is surprising about them is their sharp sense of history. In a region where space is so overpowering and the past of the white people is so short, one would expect poets to write mostly about the landscape, and often they do just that. But they also write with poignancy about the brief history of which they belong. They write of fathers and grandfathers as if they were people in ancient legends. In a moving group of poems in one of his earlier books, Dale Zieroth tells of his German grandfather, an immigrant who never bothered to become naturalized, beginning to succeed on his farm, then, when World War I begins, being taken to an internment camp, leaving his wife to cope with the children and the farm. It is the kind of story of hope and disappointment that echoes through the tales Mark Abley heard as he wandered over the country gathering the impressions that make up *Beyond Forget*. We are reminded constantly of the great surge of promise with which settlement on the prairies began, the hardships endured in the hope of a future better than anything possible in the old country, and then the dashing of hope by a war, a depression, a series of bad seasons.

I suppose it is inevitable that with short, dramatic pasts of this kind people should look back to ancestors. Some of the prairie poets, like Robert Kroetsch and Andrew Suknaski, write of the Indians who were there before history began, and adopt them as spiritual ancestors. Others, like Dale Zieroth, think of real ancestors, but in another country, and identify with them imaginatively.

Many of us feel the need for ancestors. I don't know how universal the need is, since I often meet people who claim that they have no interest in the past, and if I suspect they are lying, it is probably because I cannot think of a life without ancestors, who sometimes come alive for us in amazing ways. In his poem, Dale Zieroth not only remembers his fur-hatted ancestress on a day the soldiers are being called up, presumably for World War I, but he also sees himself there, in mental touch, so that as his poem ends he feels he is both woman and soldier, long ago:

    and now I am feeling my head, not sure
    what it is I am touching
    hair or fur

As I read these lines I was reminded of finding one of my own ancestors and, curiously, the memory is also associated with soldiers. When I was about five I was taken to the Shropshire village from which my mother's mother had come. In the garden behind the old family house I was shown a disused baking oven made of brick and fireclay in which wood was burnt and the ashes were then raked out before the bread was put in to bake. It had belonged to my great-grandmother, a very independent lady called Bessy France, and something about the way she was spoken of aroused my curiosity. As I grew older I pieced the story together through questioning my grandfather.

They were the mid-Victorian days when service in the British Army was long and hard and nobody wanted to be a Tommy Atkins. So recruiting sergeants were sent out to attend country fairs, get likely young men tipsy, and persuade them to accept what was called the "Queen's shilling" and sign themselves up, which they often regretted bitterly when they sobered up in Shrewsbury barracks. But by now they were under military law, and if they ran away it was desertion, which made them liable to appalling punishments.

One day during the Crimean war, a young man came limping into Bessy's garden, exhausted and obviously terrified. He had been plied with drink the weekend before, recruited, and a couple of days later had run away. Here was someone in distress, and Bessy did not need to ask any questions. She thought quickly, thrust him into the oven and piled wood in front of him. Not long afterwards his pursuers arrived. They searched the house and the outhouses, the stable and the barn, but they never thought of taking the wood out of the oven. When they had gone, Bessy liberated and fed the young man, gave him money and clothing, and set him on a cross-country way to a small Welsh port where he could get on a boat to Ireland and freedom. She never heard of him again, and she did not live long enough for me to know her in the flesh.

Her story made a great impression on me, and often while helping refugees, which I have done frequently during my life, I have felt that the voice of that Shropshire foremother was speaking in my head, like Dale Zieroth's Polish ancestress. We are all, more than we often think or know, what the past has made us.

THE ENVIABLE EXPATRIATE

*Though I have hardly had any public recognition, I have an
immense private following. This kind of success is not the same as
recognition. My career has all along been lucky, but I feel that I
am now at the beginning of my development, not at the end. I feel
as Hokusai did when, at the age of eighty, he said that if he could
only live ten more years he might begin to attain mastery.*

Joseph Plaskett,
Exhibition Catalogue, "The White Table"

In these essays I have never before made my text something so
apparently ephemeral as the catalogue of an art exhibition that lasted
a mere two weeks. That I do so now demonstrates my respect for the
wisdom as well as the skill of one of the best of Canadian painters.

In November 1986, Joe Plaskett made one of his rare forays from his
adopted home in Paris for an exhibition of his works in Montréal. He
came on to Vancouver and gave me the catalogue of his show, which
had followed a theme of the utmost simplicity. As its title, *The White
Table*, suggested, the paintings had a single constant element, a white
table or a table with a white cloth. On the table were varying combinations of flowers and fruit and wineglasses, and sometimes a bottle. It
was the simplest of still-life equipment, yet painted with such assurance, such luminosity and such painterly virtuosity of colouring that
one recognized the certainty of a master. Alas, as I quickly learned,
there would be no chance of my owning any of these splendid canvases
to add to my small collection of Plasketts; all but two had been sold in

the first ten minutes of the show to keen buyers, some of whom had waited nine hours on a Montreal November day on the pavement outside the gallery. It was a triumphant return of an artist to his native land.

But I did have the catalogue, with the autobiographical essay Joe had written to accompany the illustrations, and which I valued because it showed a power over words unusual in a visual artist. I admired the realistic modesty with which it showed the slow development of an artist who eventually flowered, as his great predecessor James Wilson Morrice had done, far from his native Canada. But I was also touched at times by the curious interaction of lives it displayed.

Most of the paintings in the exhibition were done in the medieval house Joe Plaskett has acquired in the Marais quarter of Paris. For reasons about which I myself am not entirely clear, I have not revisited Paris since Joe moved into that ancient house of winding staircases, though the sunlight pours into one of its rooms in a painting that hangs on my walls in Vancouver. But in his catalogue Joe describes a great salon he once rented for twelve years on the Boulevard St. Germain, "full of ghosts and the relics of a fabulous past, the setting of the dream that I was daily living," and there I had known the Parisian Joe Plaskett best, during a year from 1957 to 1958 when my wife and I were in France. Paris seemed to be full of Canadian friends that year. Poet Phyllis Webb was there, and so were painters Molly and Bruno Bobak, and we used to meet in the cafés and cheap eating houses of the Latin Quarter and sometimes in Joe's salon-studio, a remnant of *la belle époque*, with its tall French windows letting in the sunlight — silver in winter and golden in spring — and its great chandelier, which Joe succeeded in transporting to his medieval house in the Marais.

Phyllis Webb wrote a poem about that room and its gleaming chandelier, and Joe painted a splendid suite of glowing canvases catching the ever-changing Paris light and populating it with the hieratic figures of women. He has always been a painter who has found his inspiration close at hand. Not many years ago he went no farther than his mirror and did an exhibition full of penetratingly self-analytical self-portraits. Now he has gone back to the basic test of skill and sensitivity, the still life of fruits or flowers on which so many artists — Cézanne with his apples and so forth — have proved their virtuosity and their skill at the handling of paint. And have proved also that subject is irrelevant, for a dozen true artists can take the same simple bowl of fruit or vase of flowers and present a dozen entirely different images.

What interests me especially about a painter like Joe Plaskett is the way he abandoned what looked like a promising career in Canada and set off to find himself in Paris, the traditional world capital of painting. The result has been the situation he describes in the quotation I have used. He does not have the kind of public standing in Canada that painters like Jack Shadbolt and Harold Town command; Joe Plaskett is not a public Canadian figure. Yet many people passionately collect his works and privately value them. At the same time, Joe has never been accepted as a painter in Paris, where he lives. Almost a century ago, when James Wilson Morrice went to Paris and became a friend of Matisse, it was possible for a Canadian to immerse himself in the currents of Impressionism and Post-Impressionism and become accepted by the French artists almost as one of their own. Morrice exhibited in the great Paris salons and his works were bought by the French government before anyone in Canada, except William Van Horne, thought they were worth buying. It is different now. The French art world is densely populated and no longer open to strangers. So Joe Plaskett's magical paintings have received little notice in the city he has chosen to make his own.

But has he lost by this? The fineness of his paintings and the wisdom with which he writes suggest that he has not. He distanced himself from his past, he found his inspiration in what lay immediately around him, he spent time perfecting painterly skills that in Canada he might have wasted teaching art or serving on the endless juries and committees of our over-bureaucratized art world. And now, he is painting better than ever before, and still he feels "at the beginning of my development, not at the end." One can only envy this recluse with a multitude of friends who lives with the sense of an unbounded future of creation.

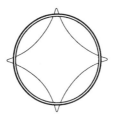

THE LAND OF LOST CONTENT

Into my heart an air that kills
From yon far country blows:
What are those blue remembered hills,
What spires, what farms are those?

A.E. Housman,
The Shropshire Lad

There are poems that stir one's myths. And the little poem I have quoted, merely numbered XL in *The Shropshire Lad*, awakens one of mine.

Everyone has his private mythologies, and some of us have several, overlapping each other. For a long time now I have seen myself as a solid citizen of British Columbia, devoted to the mountains and seacoasts of my adoptive region. But behind such local loyalties lurks a more broadly Canadian Woodcock, born in the Grace Hospital in Winnipeg and reared for a few months in a plain wooden apartment building on Portage Avenue. And behind him there stands the Shropshire Lad.

My parents were both "proud Salopians," as the saying went in the Welsh border country, and when they took me back to England it was to the Shropshire of A.E. Housman's poignant poems that we went. There I spent most of my early childhood; there, when my parents went to live in the south of England, I would still go on every school holiday, to stay with my grandparents. In those years of boyhood and adolescence I developed such an affection for the quiet and golden

Shropshire countryside that I could think of no better prospect than to live my life in the land of my ancestors. I became the perfect Shropshire Lad.

But external events play havoc with one's dearest ambitions. I left my school in the south of England in 1929, just when the Depression was beginning to freeze life in Europe. Work of any kind was almost impossible to find. My grandfather, a man of modest wealth, had his own very simple solution. One branch of our family had produced a cousin, the archdeacon, who would occasionally appear at family gatherings in his gaiters and his strange taped top hat. My grandfather, looking at my examination results, decided he might have a potential bishop to offer in competition and proposed to send me to Cambridge if I would become a clergyman. I refused, not because of any free-thinking inclinations (those came later), but from sheer timidity; I could not see myself developing the self-confidence needed to stand in a pulpit and lecture my fellow men on the will of God. In any case, all I was interested in was getting back to live in that countryside whose spell Housman cast on his generation. (Ironically, he himself was a Worcestershire, not a Shropshire lad.)

But in those Depression days there were no respectable jobs to be had in Shropshire, and the only work I could find was in London. I was lost to the "blue remembered hills." And once, when I did return at the age of twenty to my beloved Shropshire town, all those romantically remembered fragments of landscape seemed not merely less poetic, but even physically smaller, as if both my dream and the land itself had shrunk. I thought then that my childhood longings were all submerged.

It was Paris and the sun-bitten hills of Provence that called me now, and finally I returned to the land where I was born. Reaching my native Winnipeg on a bitter winter's day, I went on to the coast, and decided that was as far west as I needed to travel. I have spent the second half of my life here, and for many years thought that the Shropshire Lad was a well-laid ghost.

Yet when I started to write my first volume of autobiography, *Letter to the Past*, that ghost came shouldering back to stand beside me, and I wrote in a flood of memory, reconstructing to the last meaningful stone the Shropshire past I had thought was lost to me forever. In the hidden depths of memory it had been waiting all the time, as in the second verse of Housman's little poem:

> That is the land of lost content,
> I see it shining plain,
> The happy highways where I went
> And cannot come again.

I saw it plain indeed, as the words flowed from my fingers onto my typewriter. I lived it again, perhaps more vividly than I had ever done in the past, for the memory is a noted enhancer of colour. It was there day after day, alive in my mind's eye.

And yet could I, any more than Housman's protagonist, "come again?" Could I return physically to the countryside I was now remembering so intensely? I thought of going back, and even made my preparations, but at the last moment I abandoned the idea. For I knew I would not be seeing the country I had once known and now remembered. It was not merely that in all those years it would have changed, with towns rebuilt, and great old country houses pulled down, and highways where once there had been winding lanes, and the poppies driven away from the wheat-fields with herbicide and the butterflies driven away from the hedgerows with pesticide.

It was the change in me as much as in the land that I would have to contend with. I could no longer go back and see it again through the eyes of a fifteen-year-old awakening to the poetry of life. The Shropshire Lad had indeed lived on in the depths of memory and emerged to stand beside me when I called him up. But memory and present perception are two different things, and I knew that if I went back to Shropshire, it would be my aging self, loaded with the experience of far travels, who would look at it and judge its real modesty. But I knew also that the vision lived on in the deep recesses of my mind. By keeping it away, I could still see it "shining plain" through the eyes of the Shropshire Lad.

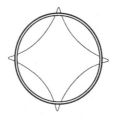

POEMS TO BE
SEEN AND HEARD

The iron rocks
slope sharply down
into the gleaming
of northern water,
and there is a shining
to northern water
reflecting the sky
on a keen cool morning.

W.W.E. Ross,
"*Rocky Bay*"

The lakeshore cottage has been a traditional feature of Canadian summer life ever since the railway reached the Muskoka Lakes in the 1870s, and the many sheets of fresh water in the hollows of the Canadian Shield and the valleys of British Columbia have become the centres of hot-weather cultures that inevitably have found their way into Canadian novels and stories, from Ethel Wilson's *Swamp Angel* to Margaret Atwood's *Surfacing*. More distant and solitary lakes provided the land and waterscapes that inspired Tom Thomson and the Group of Seven, the first consciously national movement in the Canadian visual arts.

But they also offered the images that inspired much of the early modern poetry that began to appear in Canada during the 1920s. The first real Canadian modernist poet was W.W.E. Ross, whose *Laconics* appeared in 1930 and whose poem "Rocky Bay," about an Ontario lakeshore, I quoted above. Others followed his example with lakeside poems that are now among our literary classics, like A.J.M. Smith's "The Lonely Land," with its central image of a black pine by a lake, which seemed like a verbal echo of Thomson's famous painting *The West Wind*, and F.R. Scott's "Lakeshore," which begins with a verse like a variation of Ross's poem:

> The lake is sharp along the shore
> Trimming the bevelled edge of land
> To level curves; the fretted sands
> Go slanting down through liquid air
> Till stones below shift here and there
> Floating upon their broken sky
> All netted by the prism wave
> And rippled where the currents are.

These early Canadian poets were very much under the influence of the movement known as Imagism, whose leading figures were Ezra Pound and the American poet Hilda Doolittle, who wrote under her initials, H.D. The idea of Imagist poetry was that the poem should centre on a precise image, usually visual, and that the image, if it were sensitively offered, would suggest its own emotional associations without the poet having to draw them to the reader's attention. It was a kind of poetry especially fitted to a land like Canada, which was opening up territorially and offering fascinating new visual experiences.

In fact, though Imagism was an international movement, its earliest origins can be traced in Canada. The first of all the Imagists was an English poet named T.E. Hulme, who in 1912 published a group of five short poems made up of carefully ordered and precise images which he called *The Complete Poetical Works of T.E. Hulme*, a title that was ironically exact, because Hulme was killed in Flanders in 1917. But the interesting fact for Canadian readers is that Hulme spent eight months in 1906 and 1907 wandering over Canada doing casual work on farms and in lumber camps. It was the visual aspects of Canada that appealed to him, and after he returned to Britain and began to write under the encouragement of his friend Ezra Pound, he said: "Speaking of personal matters, the first time I ever felt the necessity or inevitableness of verse, was in the desire to reproduce the peculiar quality of feeling which is induced by the flat spaces and wide horizons of the virgin prairie of western Canada." Certainly Canadian poets, writing in the decade after Hulme's death, found in a poetry starting from images a way to break away from the romantic kind of nature poetry, using Victorian forms, that had been written by men like Archibald Lampman and Bliss Carman at the turn of the century, and to develop a new kind of verse that seemed appropriate to Canadian experience.

Not all the poets who followed W.W.E. Ross and F.R. Scott wrote Imagist poetry or anything like it. Many of them have been concerned much more with sound patterns than with images, and have tried to relate poetry to speech rather than to sight. In trying to explain this, I have come to the conclusion that there are two different kinds of perception involved in poetry and probably in other forms of writing. Some people are visualizers, and what they read immediately creates pictorial images in their minds; as a result, they often have difficulty with abstract concepts, which they cannot visualize. I recognize myself as one of this type. Others are much more concerned with the cadences of the writing, and tend to hear rather than to see what they read. You can recognize them among poets as those who are always relating poetry to music.

Still, probably no poet is entirely visual or entirely audial. If you look again at the quotation from W.W.E. Ross, you will see that, though it does not have a regular metrical structure, there are underlying cadences which emerge when you read it aloud, and which are reinforced by echo (the phrase "northern water" is repeated) and by the half-echo of a kind of irregular rhyming — "gleaming," "shining," "morning." And so we must probably conclude that while paintings, like Victorian children, should be seen and not hear, poetry should ideally be both seen in the mind's eye and heard in the mind's ear.

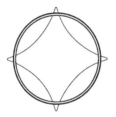

NYMPHS AND TRANSFORMERS

> My purpose is to tell of bodies which have been transformed into shapes of a different kind. You heavenly powers, since you were responsible for these changes, look favorably on my efforts.

Ovid,
The Metamorphoses

Metamorphosis is a powerful myth and in nature a powerful fact. I shall never forget how, more than seventy years ago, aged five, I was introduced by two eight-year-old entomologists, who kept caterpillars in big glass jars full of greenery, to the mysterious cycle by which a worm with many legs turned first into an apparently lifeless mummylike chrysalis, whose paper integument in time broke apart to release a Red Admiral, which flapped its feeble wings to dry and eventually flew magnificently away. It created a wonder in me that has made natural history a lifelong flirtation — if not a major passion — ever since.

Ovid, one of the early writers of Imperial Rome, was better known for *The Art of Love*, a cynical little treatise on the ways of seduction, than for *The Metamorphoses*, the ambitious work on the role of metamorphosis in mythology that he completed when a prudish Caesar Augustus exiled him to the Black Sea for his amorous poems. But, in the long run, *The Metamorphoses* seems the more interesting work, as Ovid takes us into a strange world that has become familiar to twentieth-century man because of the importance we know primitive peoples attach to transformation myths.

Transformation is a perpetual theme in the legends of Canadian

Indians, for example, and some of the most dramatic of the winter dances of the Kwakiutl in British Columbia were those in which the ingenious transformation masks were used, the head of an eagle or a bear, operated by invisible strings, suddenly opening to reveal the humanoid face of the spirit that had assumed the animal form. The Greeks and the Romans were much nearer primitive man than European man has since become. Like the West Coast shamanists or African animists, they believed that the whole natural world was inhabited by spirits that could, like the Coast Indians' Salmon King, take on human shape when needed. A nymph, for example, *was* the vital principle of a tree or a spring and hence indistinguishable from it. But she could also appear, as a god or goddess could, in human form, to tempt or threaten mere mortals.

Classical legends include a whole series of such romantically appealing transformations: lustful old Pan pursuing the nymph called Syrinx, who is saved by being transformed into a reed, from which the god resourcefully makes his panpipes; lustful young Apollo chasing a nymph named Daphne, and she being transformed into a laurel tree, whose branches Apollo uses to make the crowns that honour distinguished men. The blood of Hyacinthus, killed in a sporting accident, becomes the flower that bears his name, and the blood of Adonis, gored by a wild bear, turns into anemones. Though I found in Lebanon — where the Adonis legend originated — that the actual name *adonis* was given not to those splendid flowers that encrimsoned the limestone hills around Baalbek, but to a herb like chevril that was mashed into a salad. Still, the idea of regeneration as well as transformation was there. The slain hero in the true tradition of fertility myths was transformed into and commemorated by something rising lushly from the earth.

What Ovid did was to try and bring together all these myths into a kind of system showing all parts of nature to be interchangeable. The idea that gods could transform themselves into men, and nymphs into plants, and that men — by the intervention of a witch called Circe — could turn into swine and other beasts became for him the evidence of a vast interconnecting pattern in which all forms of life were dependent on each other. Centuries later, during the Renaissance and the time of early scientific pioneers, the idea of the interdependence of life reemerged in the concept of the Great Chain of Being, which extended from God to the most infinitesimal creatures. As Alexander Pope put it in his *Essay on Man* (1734):

> Vast chain of being! which from God began;
> Natures ethereal, human, angel, man,
> Beast, bird, fish, insect, who no eye can see,
> No glass can reach; from infinite to thee;
> From thee to nothing . . .

But this chain was seen as a hierarchical order, God at the top and the creatures made visible by the newly invented microscope at the bottom.

The revolutions in thought that have taken place more recently bring us much nearer to the ancients, and to primitive people; now the concept of ecosystem has replaced hierarchy with the idea of mutual interdependence. We need the birds and the bees because our world would go wrong without them, and the feeling that man is in some way the equal of other creatures, and not their master, comes back into our hearts. In this sense, while metamorphosis exists actually in the transformations of insects and amphibians and even the human foetus, it begins to take on a broader, metaphorical character. We get from it the idea of changing places mentally with other creatures, and so we are led towards a closer understanding of them. Carried too far, of course, that can be self-deceptive. As wise Montaigne once remarked: "When I play with my cat, who knows that she is not amusing herself more with me than I with her?"

The terms of our interdependence with other creatures, plants or animals, will always be elusive; it is difficult enough to enter the minds of other humans, let alone other species. Yet the sense of a sympathetic continuity between us and other living creatures, emphasized in Buddhism and Hinduism, is necessary, and the value of myths of transformation, in which identities are seen as mutable and men *may* change into plants or animals, lies in their power to stir our imaginations. It is by imagining that we develop our empathies, so that, even if we are not transformed into reeds or laurel trees, we acquire the power to undergo our metamorphoses in metaphor.

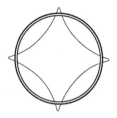

SANDS OF TIME,
WINDS OF CHANGE

At the foot of the mountain range lay the old travel road, wide and deeply marked, literally cut to bits by the sharp nail-studded wheels of countless caravan carts . . . . Over this road myriads of travellers had journeyed for thousands of years, making it a cease- lessly flowing stream of life, for it was the great highway of Asia, which connected the Far East with distant European lands.

Mildred Cable,
The Gobi Desert

Thanks to one of life's happy synchronicities, just on the eve of a recent trip to China, my wife and I looked in on a bookseller friend, and there on her desk, the newest arrival, lay a reprint of *The Gobi Desert*. Mildred Cable and two other indefatigable English missionary ladies set out in 1923 for the Gobi desert and spent years recrossing it, starting in the arid province of Kansu and exploring the hinterlands of Mongolia and Sinkiang (Chinese Turkestan); indeed, they were the first European women to travel in the Gobi.

Mildred and her companions, Eva and Francesca French, were singularly unbiased Christians, eager to meet the monks and priests in remote desert temples and to stress the common elements in religion rather than the peculiar virtues of Christianity. Because of this they were welcomed wherever they went, and the news of these tough steel-spectacled ladies, bundled in their padded Chinese garb, spread through the desert. The three women were the last of a line of great travellers who wandered in traditional ways, by cart or on the backs of shaggy Bactrian camels, over the great stretches of the Silk Road that led through the desolate wastes and mountains of Central Asia to unite the production centres of China with markets for oriental products in Europe, Persia, India.

The Greek philosopher Aristotle mentioned silk from Cathay in the fourth century B.C. A piece of early Chinese fabric was found in the South German tomb of a Scythian warrior from two centuries before that. But the first great account of a journey over the Silk Road was that of the Buddhist monk Hsuan Tsang, who in the seventh century A.D. went on a long journey to India, which took him eighteen years, and brought him back with an invaluable store of Buddhist writings. Hsuan Tsang's journey achieved legendary status in China, where it was linked with the story of the mythical Monkey King, who was said to have aided him on this incredible journey.

After Hsuan Tsang came Marco Polo, who dictated in a Genoese prison the story of his journey along the Silk Road to visit Kublai Khan in the late thirteenth century. His greatest successor was the archaeologist Aurel Stein, who went on four notable expeditions to the Silk Road between 1900 and 1930 and revealed an extraordinary series of lost cities drifted over by the sands of the Gobi and the Takla Makan deserts. His *On Central Asian Tracks* was another of the books we took in our baggage as we set out on our own journey.

Vast stretches of the Silk Road are unchanged today, half a century and more after Mildred Cable last travelled it. Sand dunes and pebbly desert tufted with tamarisk bushes are framed to the south by the great snow mountains of the Qiliang Shan, and to the north by the bright volcanic peaks of the Longshou Shan beyond which lies Mongolia. For much of the way, almost as far as the great Buddhist cave temples of Dunhuang, one is in sight of the remnants of the Great Wall: not the reconstructed masonry barrier one visits near Peking, but a wall of mud held together by twig fascines, built in the Han dynasty two millennia ago. The everlasting wind has wrought more damage to it than the hordes of northern barbarians against whom it was built ever did, and in some places it is worn almost level with the ground, but in other places there are still massive tawny remnants of gates and watchtowers.

Standing beside them in that empty, windy waste, one remembers the poignant old Chinese poems about the exile of military service on the Great Wall.

We travelled the Silk Road from Lanzhou at its beginning to Dun-huang, a distance of about 1200 kilometres, in two long and exhausting days. It would have taken more than two months when Mildred Cable and her companions first set out; mud ruins by the roadside marked the sites of the old deserted caravanserais, situated about 24 kilometres apart, a night's walk for a camel or a bullock cart. A few Bactrian camels survive on the Road. We saw some, looking disreputably shabby because their thick winter pelts fell off in patches with the onset of spring, but they merely drew local carts. Truck traffic had already begun before Mildred Cable left the Gobi, and so had the trains running through to Turfan and Urumchi in Sinkiang. They, too, evoke their own kind of nostalgia, for China is one of the few countries not only using but also still manufacturing steam locomotives, massive giants that burn low-grade coal and can be seen far over the desert ejecting their impressive black plumes of smoke against the jagged mountains.

But the Silk Road is even now not all trucks and trains. In its old towns, like Wuwei and Zhangye and Jiuquan, with their crumbling city walls and their Ming bell towers, their wooden temples from the Sung dynasty wonderfully preserved in the desert air, there is a sense of the long historic past behind the bustle of the free markets in the main streets, where another kind of old China, that of the traders and traffickers, is reviving in the current atmosphere of economic reform.

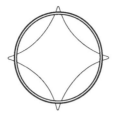

A CHANGE OF HEART

It is hard to explain the fascination of Canada geese. I do not hunt primarily to kill them, but to be concerned with them. I am relieved rather than disappointed when the flock rises just beyond range, swings wide, or passes high; I love their name, their long black necks, the clean white cheek patches, the strong and heavy bodies.

Roderick Haig-Brown,
Measure of the Year.

The relationship between hunters and their quarry is often a complex one. There are indeed those single-minded beings who are moved only by an economical need to fill a freezer or by a simple love of killing. But perhaps they are fewer than one thinks; perhaps many hunters share the complexity of response that Haig-Brown displayed when he wrote of hunting duck and geese at the head of inlets on Vancouver Island, where he lived. Haig-Brown continues the passage I have just quoted: "They mean courage to me, devotion, wisdom, endurance, and beauty, and I care not at all that the first three of these attributes should not normally be applied to creatures less than man." And then, at the end of the paragraph, he adds: "In cold reason, it seems fantastic to consider their destruction by gunshot; yet every emotion I feel from them is strengthened and deepened, at the moment and in recollection, by carrying a gun."

It does seem a strange, contradictory combination of attitudes, but I find it interesting because in a rather striking way it links one of the most complex of Canadian writers with the Indian peoples who hunted over the same terrain before the white man came on the scene. Rod Haig-Brown was one of those writers with a double reputation: an international one, and a very different local one. His books on fishing — *Fisherman's Spring, Fisherman's Summer*, and so forth — gained him an enormous following among sports fishermen throughout North America, and his home near Campbell River on the north-eastern shore of Vancouver Island was a place of pilgrimage where they would arrive in large numbers. But Rod was not merely a fisherman's writer, or a hunter's writer. He was also a writer's writer, a master of fluent prose, and perhaps the best Canadian example of the kind of nature writer — like W.H. Hudson and Richard Jefferies — who flourished in Britain before the countryside became too filled with houses.

Rod wrote fiction, but the form he loved best was the reflective and descriptive essay. The essay, which enjoyed such a vogue in the nineteenth century when it was handled by masters like Charles Lamb and William Hazlitt, has fallen out of favour in recent years with the general public, but professional writers still regard it as a testing literary exercise. Perhaps because our vast country cries out for description, and for reflection on the descriptions, Canadian writers have been inclined to write essays. Frederick Philip Grove's essays, *Over Prairie Trails*, were better than any of his ponderous novels, and many critics have made similar comparisons between Hugh MacLennan's essays and his fiction; indeed, they have often said that his novels are best understood as fictional essays putting forth points of view about the destiny of Canada. His fellow writers — and I remember that MacLennan agreed with me on this — ranked Haig-Brown high as an essayist, especially for his great book on the Canadian seasons, *Measure of the Year*, but also, surprisingly enough, for many of the essays on fishing.

Rod Haig-Brown did not confine himself to being a writer. He acted as magistrate in his own community, a terror to those who shot protected birds and compassionate to drunkards and petty thieves. He served on government commissions. He was chancellor of the University of Victoria. I used to remonstrate with him and argue that he should be cultivating his unique talents as a writer. Rod would suck on his pipe and give a soft, wise answer. Afterward I realized he was not a compelled writer like me. He wrote to say things that were important to him, but if he could express himself in action, that was just as good so far as he was concerned.

He solved the contradiction in his attitude to hunted animals as much by action as by words. Hunting had given Rod a sense of identification with the outdoors through which he roamed, and eventually a feeling of kinship with the quarry he had observed so carefully. But for modern man who need not hunt in order to live, the sense of kinship with the animal can no longer be assuaged by killing and then carrying out, like a primitive hunter, some propitiatory ceremony to the spirit of the beast.

There must be some form of identification short of destruction, and by the time I knew him, in the late 1950s, Rod Haig-Brown had already given up hunting animals and birds. He preferred to observe and write about them. He still fished, for somehow, in their different element, fish did not inspire the same feeling of kinship as warm-blooded animals. Then he began to scuba dive in the river outside his house, where up to now he had fished. As he explored the depths day after day, he began to recognize the inhabitants individually. He would see a big fish that liked to shelter beside a particular rock; it would be there every day, and a sense of friendship would grow up. It was no longer a cold-blooded creature under the mirror surface of the water. It was another denizen of a place which Rod now partially inhabited. He could not possibly go back on the bank and let down a lure to drag it out of its hiding spot. And so, a little while before the day he died cultivating his garden beside the river, Rod had given up fishing, too.

He had recognized that civilization had changed man so that he was no longer a predator among other predators; it had changed the terms of the kinship between men and animals as it had changed the terms of the kinship between men. If we no longer accept war as a true manifestation of the relations between men and men, we must also examine our assumption that our relationship with the animals allows us to destroy them. There are more ways of hunting than the one that leads to death.

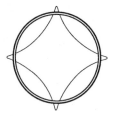

WINTERS OF CONTENT

Now is the winter of our discontent
Made glorious summer by this son of York.

> William Shakespeare,
> *Richard III*

Unlike halts in summer, winter sojourns bear a kind of honorary
citizenship.

> Patrick Leigh Fermor,
> *A Time for Gifts*

Patrick Leigh Fermor is a travel writer whose books I have always
enjoyed, but it was only recently that I read *A Time of Gifts*, which is
a book about his travels before he ever thought of making his living by
writing about them. At the age of eighteen, Fermor set off from a
London dock on a rainy December day in 1933 with the intent of
finding his way on foot through Europe from the Hook of Holland to
Constantinople, as he still archaically called Istanbul. The journey
turned out to be so full of incident and impression that, when Fermor
sat down to write it from memory and fragmentary diaries forty years
later, he found he had finished a whole volume before he got beyond
the frontiers of Hungary into the Balkans.

What he offers is a splendid picture of Germany during the last shaky
days of the Weimar Republic, with the passions of Nazism rising to the

88

boiling point and already spilling over into Austria. He set off in a mid-winter month that only the quixotic would choose for a tramp through central Europe, and he saw the charms of the Rhineland and Bavaria, of Upper Austria and Bohemia and Hungary largely veiled in snow or lashed by rain. But the very inhospitability of the land inevitably made him more anxious for human hospitality, for the shelter and warmth of inns and youth hostels, for the occasional islands of grace when he found himself under the roof of some Central European aristocrat of decayed fortune but treasured lifestyle.

It was this entry to foreign homes and hearths, given with amazing generosity and warmth at a time when nationalist passions were rising up everywhere on the continent of Europe, that led Fermor to make the remark I have quoted. Because he was not one of the familiar horde of summer tourists, or of fair-weather *Wandervogel*, and was always turning up alone, lost, cold, hungry, or soaked to the skin, he aroused the friendly feelings of a host of people, and, even though he was once robbed and occasionally threatened, he felt taken into the heart of a continent in a way that could never have happened in the smiling days of summer. And so he remarks on the "honorary citizenship" that one acquires in sojourns on winter travels.

What he says accords with my experience. Whenever I have had cause to live away from home for an extended period in the northern hemisphere, I have always chosen to do so in winter. This is partly because it is cheaper, and partly because one exchanges the social extroversion of summer for the social introversion of winter. Towns close in upon themselves, and if you are living in a foreign place at such a season it is much easier to feel oneself a part of its life. You move daily among the townspeople, conspicuous and yet, in a curious way, accepted and perceived, while in summer you would be exploited and — as a human being rather than a spending machine — ignored. After two or three weeks the shopkeepers know you and give you fair weight; after two or three meals in a restaurant the waiter greets you and tells you which dishes to avoid.

Still, there are differences in winter sojourns, depending on the kind of town one chooses to stay in. In the large cities of Europe, like Zurich or Munich or Vienna, it is the season for great cultural events, for opera and theatre, concerts and major art exhibitions, and uproarious public festivals. The city does not condescend to give such entertainments to its summer visitors, who are incidental to its real life. In winter it seems to shake them off like a dog shaking fleas and resume its own collective dream-life; wise is the stranger who immerses himself in it unobtrusively, as if he were an "honorary citizen."

Winters in resort towns are different. There a kind of hibernation takes place. Hotels are closed or scantily populated. Parks, lakefronts, or sea promenades are deserted, and with their bare trees and flowerless gardens project the mood of diffused melancholy that is beloved of solitary walkers. But in the real hearts of these towns, like Lugano and Locarno on the Swiss lakes, or in the narrow lanes around the ports at places on the Côte d'Azur like Menton and Nice, the residual garrison of local inhabitants carry on their lives as ever before. The half-empty restaurants are patronized only by local people, and the food is correspondingly better than it is during the high season. Such entertainment as goes on lacks the lavish vulgarity of summer, and often turns out to be of discreetly good quality, like the fine baroque concert — Handel and Haydn, Stradella and Corelli and Vivaldi — that we heard last St. Sebastian's Day (Boxing Day to Canadians) in a baroque church of superb acoustics in the old town of Locarno, attended — apart from ourselves — entirely by the Locarnesi. Such communities draw together when the tourists have gone, and the odd winter visitor comes into direct contact with the local life that tends to be submerged during the tourist season. If he has been to the place for more than one winter, he finds himself tracing alterations in mood and makeup.

Last winter, for example, revisiting the towns of Ticino, where we had spent a winter nineteen years ago, I was intrigued by a change in the Ticinese manner. The people had been aloof and shy and somewhat dour in comparison with their fellow Lombards over the border in Italy. Two decades years later I found them strikingly changed, more "Italian" in their freedom of manner, friendlier to strangers and even curious about them. Was this a result of the opening of their eyes to the world that the spread of television had brought about over the past two decades? Whatever the cause, it made me feel more than ever drawn into the honorary citizenship of winter of which Fermor speaks, and which, if it does not turn that season into the summer of Shakespeare's lines, at least transforms it into a winter of content.

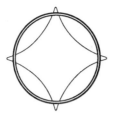

AND A HAPPY LI PO TO YOU

And Li Po also died drunk.
He tried to embrace a moon
In the Yellow River.

Ezra Pound,
Lustra

By fortunate chance I celebrated my last birthday beside the Yellow River, or, rather, my Chinese friends celebrated it, for that night they offered me a small banquet, with suckling pig and lamb cooked in chafing dishes in the Gobi desert manner and many other northern Chinese dishes. And, remembering I was a poet, they offered me a potent rice spirit called Happy Li Po, in an elegant porcelain jar on which the poet was represented, joyfully striding under the flowering peach trees in his long silk gown of the T'ang period with his hair flowing out tumultuously under his court headdress.

I enjoyed the gesture as well as the *aqua vitae*, for I had been reading Li Po's poems for many years. I was happy to find on reaching China that, after all the vicissitudes of the Cultural Revolution, when his works were dismissed along with all the manifestations of the old culture, he is now in favour again; in fact, he is probably the most popular of the classic poets among Chinese readers. As a very young poet in the 1920s I had shared in the revelation of a different view of poetry which the discovery of the T'ang poets meant to writers like Ezra Pound. What was it that intrigued us about these people who wrote twelve-hundred years ago and in a distant land? What affinities did we recognize over the centuries and the oceans and the desert highways that linked Li Po's China with our so different world?

I think the answer is quite simple. The old Chinese poets helped to give English and American poets in the early part of this century a new outlook on their art by teaching them the importance of the image.

Interest in oriental cultures — *Chinoiserie* and *Japonoiserie* — had already influenced Western visual artists by the late nineteenth century. Both the French Impressionists and the American cosmopolitan James McNeill Whistler were inspired by Japanese woodblock prints and by Chinese painting from the Sung era. The impact of visual arts on minds open to new experience is always immediate. The impact of poetry, which depends on translation, is slower, but by the turn of the century Western writers like Lafcadio Hearn and Ernest Francisco Fenollosa were immersing themselves in Asian cultures, and it was through reading the notes on Chinese poetry which Fenollosa left on his death in 1908 that Pound became one of the first Western poets to present versions of Chinese verse, in a book called *Cathay* (1915). These were not translations, since Pound knew little if any Chinese, but brilliant renderings.

Pound and his contemporaries were seeking an escape from the rhetorical poetry of the Victorian age, which depends more on vague words and misty abstract concepts than on clearly heard sound and clearly seen images. In the work of Li Po and his contemporaries, they found a poetry that depended greatly on the pictures it created in the mind's eye. Like most other poets, the T'ang writers projected such emotions as love and a feeling for the natural world, but they were most admired when they created a scene in the mind and allowed the reader to infer the emotions associated with it. Consider "The Grief of the Jade Stairs":

> A white dew grows on the jade stairs.
> When night comes, it wets her silk shoes.
> She comes in, lets fall the crystal screen,
> And gazes through it at the autumn moon.

So far as explicit statement is concerned, that is as voiceless as a mime. But the evocative images load it with implication, and we are deeply moved by the woman's sorrow, which is not even mentioned.

I have always thought that the Chinese developed this kind of poetry because they never had an audially united language, and when at last I got to China, I found that poets agreed with me. Cantonese sounds entirely different from Mandarin, and so on throughout the various regions. But Chinese has a single system of writing, and that system is pictorial, words being suggested by characters that were originally little sketches intended to evoke visually what they represented. Images can be understood even if sounds cannot, and so the Chinese can speak many languages and read only one, whose meaning lies in the visual symbols that are its characters. That is why Chinese poetry can appeal so directly, even in translation. It engages our eyes as well as our ears. Take a poem of deceptive simplicity by Li Po:

> Tomorrow the courier leaves for the frontier.
> All night she spends mending his coat.
> Diligently her fingers ply the cold needle,
> But the scissors are even colder.
> Then at last it is finished.
> The coat is handed over.
> How many days will it take to reach Lin-tao?

All is masterly indirection. The courier is leaving for the frontier, and we assume he will carry the coat to the woman's husband, stationed on the Great Wall, but the husband is never mentioned. We watch the woman working, and everything builds up through the series of images and their associations — a needle for mending and scissors for cutting, both hinting at their relationship. The husband's absence is indicated not by a statement but by a question — "How many days?" The woman's emotions are never described. They do not need to be, for we have felt them all the more poignantly because of the poem's restraint.

Li Po had an uncanny sense of projecting his mind into those of women, and some of his most poignant poems were sensitive evocations of the feelings of young girls. Yet he was in many ways a very masculine figure, a big man with a loud and raucous voice, a good swordsman and flute-player, a gargantuan eater and drinker. He was born in the frontier area of Kansu of a line of outlaws, and he himself was imprisoned three times. Yet he could write with extraordinary tenderness of flowers and women and friendship. One of my favourites among his poems is a farewell to a friend, in which the visual elements of a scene are used to reinforce the sense of loss:

> The green mountain lies beyond the north wall of the city,
> Where the white water winds to the east:
> Here we part.
> The solitary sail will attempt a flight of a thousand li,
> The flowing clouds are the dream of a wandering son.
> The setting sun, the affection of an old friend.
> So you go, waving your hands —
> Only the bark of a deer.

Whether Li Po really did die drunk, trying to embrace the moon in the Yellow River, is by no means certain. Another story tells that he was supping in his boat by moonlight when the Taoist immortals appeared and led him away riding on the back of a dolphin to the palaces of heaven. Whichever story you accept, there is moonlight and water, and while he was alive Li Po wrote many poems about drinking in moonlight. One of my favourites is a whimsical one that begins thus:

> Holding a jug of wine among the flowers,
> And drinking alone, not a soul keeping me company,
> I raise my cup and invite the moon to drink with me,
> And together with my shadow we are three.
> But the moon does not know the joy of drinking
> And my shadow only follows me about.

On my birthday beside the Yellow River I made a fourth in the party and drank to Li Po and his moon and his shadow.

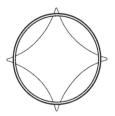

WHEN THE YEAR USED TO END

The autumn always gets me badly, as it breaks into colours. I want to go south, where there is no autumn, where the cold doesn't crouch. The heart of the North is dead, and the fingers are corpse fingers.

D.H. Lawrence

I came across this letter from D.H. Lawrence to John Middleton Murry at the height of the most splendid fall in West Coast memory. A long bright summer of blue skies and warm sunlight had so conditioned the leaves that an unexampled range of richness of colours appeared; shades and tints ranged through all the reds and yellows, the rusts and russets, and vermilions and carmines and oranges in a multichromatic feast of light; even the dull days were illumined by the brightness under the clouds. During the last days of October, Vancouverites clogged the streets and held up the traffic, driving at 30 kilometres an hour to appreciate the splendour of their city of trees.

I am writing in a very different mood from Lawrence, whose long bout with consumption perhaps explains that compulsive desire for sun and warmth which dominated the last years of his short life. I have never seen the autumn in that way. I have seen its colour always as a kind of promise, and if I write of its splendour now, as that splendour is fading, it is at least partly because I know this piece may appear in winter, when we all need assurance that the sun and warmth are not to be forgotten.

It was, as well as a splendid autumn, an unusually active Halloween in our part of the city, with more children, more originality in costume, more racket of fireworks, and the thin mists drifting in the streets heavy with gunpowder smoke. The little ghosts and witches were merry and gay (I use the word obstinately in its original expressive connotation), except for one grave pair of girls who came chained together and dressed in convict clothes; they had taken Amnesty's message to heart and carried a collecting box for Prisoners of Conscience, those living spectres of our tortured age.

Was it the splendid autumn that set off such activity? Or a reaction against the days of sunlit gloom created by the October stock market crisis? I like to think of it rather as one of those periodic returns to tradition on which, in their wisdom, the young from time to time embark. For the traditions of Halloween are very ancient and link us to the long past of our peoples in many ways. Long before the Catholic Church tried to sanitize it by making it a festival of the Saints (or Hallows), it was the great Celtic feast. It marked the end of the year, which, for the pagans, took place with the fall, when they saw the year dying in splendid colours like the breeding salmon; the new year started bleakly with bare-boughed November. Not only did great fires burn to celebrate the death of the old year. As Sir James Frazer explained in that great compendium of custom and mythology, *The Golden Bough*, Halloween was also "the time of year when the souls of the departed were supposed to revisit their old homes in order to warm themselves by the fire and to comfort themselves with the good cheer provided for them . . . by their affectionate kinsfolk." With us it is no longer the real dead who come to receive their food, but the children who come as surrogate ghosts and witches to exact their dues of candy. What was once serious belief has metamorphosed into play.

In Mexico people adhere more strictly to the past. Mexicans have been highly conscious of death ever since the Aztecs, and they call November 1 *El Dia de Los Muertos* — the Day of the Dead. For weeks before it, little chocolate coffins and sugar skulls are sold in the markets, but the great event of the day takes place after dark in the cemetery. As you enter, that usually bleak and neglected place looks like a garden of luminous flowers from the ghost lights of the candles placed on all the graves, on which the living families have spread out nocturnal picnics where they offer food to the attendant dead and sit drinking to them and reminiscing about them. In this way a sense of family continuity is preserved, and death, which the Mexicans regard so realistically, now assumes an air of unreality: St. Paul's outcry — "grave, where is thy victory?" — seems to take on point when one is feasting — even imaginatively — with the dead.

Having been brought up in England, I had not experienced Halloween in childhood, for it is little celebrated south of Hadrian's Wall. It was the Scots who made it popular in Canada. If the Catholic church tried to get rid of the pagan rule of the ghosts by substituting saints unsuccessfully, the Protestant ascendancy in England distrusted the saints just as much. But the popular desire for a celebration of autumn could not be suppressed, so it was turned into a political occasion and pushed five days farther on, to November 5, when the pagan festival was adapted to commemorate the frustration of the Gunpowder Plot in which, in 1605, Guy Fawkes had planned to blow up the House of Commons while Parliament was in session. We did not have ghosts and witches on Guy Fawkes Day, but we did spend weeks piling up junk for vast bonfires, and for days ahead of the festival we would trundle around the streets old prams loaded with rough effigies in ragged suits with round heads of rags painted with eyes, mouths, and pointed beards. "Penny for the old Guy, guv'nor!" we would shout, and spend the money we gathered to let off fireworks while we danced as wildly around the bonfire as the witches who were never mentioned. Old Nick, one felt, could never be far away.

One of the great functions of a festival like Halloween, I suppose, is that it trivializes the demonic, so that we are less inclined to blame our faults and errors on external evil forces, but to realize that we contain our own darkness as well as our own light.

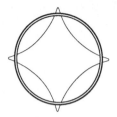

THE END OF CAGES

Only words
can fly for you like birds
on the wall of the sun.
A bird is a poem
that talks of the end of cages.

Patrick Lane,
"The Bird"

Patrick Lane is considered to be one of the most interesting of Canadian poets for his extraordinary self-generated and self-sustained achievement. By now, academic opportunities are so widespread that few people intelligent enough to show poetic promise escape the academic dragnet. Yet the escapees, who learn directly from experience and teach themselves the craft painfully, often turn out in the end to be the strongest of our poets. These include Al Purdy, Alden Nowlan, and Milton Acorn. And Pat Lane, who received little formal education and started out in a variety of menial and manual jobs that brought him to see life with a hard clarity that did not preclude compassion. Life, he saw, was difficult for human beings, but even more so for animals when men treated them unimaginatively.

His early poems were work poems, poems about the perilous life of the streets and highways, with an occasional prison scene thrown in. As he matured, he travelled a long way through the Americas, north and south, though I am not aware that he went beyond the continent until quite recently, when he travelled to China, so that to anyone with a European background his vision seems curiously focused. For him the ancient world is not Greece; it is the Peru of the Incas.

What emerges is a vision of the world just as grandly tragic as that of anyone brought up among the historic battlegrounds and graveyards of the Old World. In some ways Lane is a romantic, as poets who come so directly from among the people often are. A love poem ends poignantly:

> turn out the light
> she said and when I
> made no move to move
> my eyes to blackness
> and the loss she said
> please . . .
> so quietly my mind
> shut out the sight
> and I was blind to
> her but O the night

Or at times he becomes a kind of poetic natural philosopher. In a piece called "The Measure," dedicated to his fellow poet P.K. Page, he asks by what measure should we judge life?

> The poor, the broken people, the endless suffering
> we are heir to; given to desire and gaining little.
> To fold the arms across the breast and fly
> into ourselves. That painless darkness or stand
>
> in the field with nothing everywhere and watch
> the first flakes falling and pray for the deliverance
> of the grass, a god's death in the snow?

Shall we become involved in the problems of mankind? Shall we retreat into the ivory tower? Shall we see our fate as part of nature, where animals and men are equal?

Lane has been working on themes like this for a long time, and he has a habit, which he shares with other Canadian poets, of publishing every few years what he calls a *Selected Poems*. It does not have the finality of a *Collected Poems*, which declares one a literary monument. But it does enable one to combine recent poems, which may be few in number, with the best of one's past in a volume that has a lot of newness. Each *Selected* also leaves out a few of the poems from the past, and the reader finds as much interest in recognizing what old poems remain as in finding out what new ones are added.

The poem I quoted at the beginning of this article, "The Bird," is a favourite of mine, and I was glad to find it opening Lane's *Selected Poems* (Oxford University Press, 1987). It is addressed to a son who has caught a bird, and fostered it, and found it dying in his hands. Lane takes this pathetic incident and turns it into a metaphor for poetry. What he is really saying is that birds and poems both need freedom to fly.

> A bird is a poem
> that talks of the end of cages.

Many of Lane's poems are about birds and animals. Especially he writes of the cruelties that come from man's greed or his sheer inability to see himself in an animal's place, as a victim instead of a victor. In this sense many of Lane's poems belong to an old tradition, that of the bestiary. In ancient times, in both Europe and Asia, it was customary to embody human characteristics in animals. The fox was cunning, the lion was brave, the serpent was wise or sometimes treacherous, the elephant was patient and enduring. Whole illustrated manuscripts with splendid illuminations were devoted to delineating these characteristics, and there is an absorbing recent book, *Animals with Human Faces: A Guide to Animal Symbolism*, by Beryl Rowland, that assembles stories from the ancient bestiaries.

Nowadays we are neither so simple-minded nor so systematic in finding animal counterparts for human characteristics as earlier people. But we are still inclined to see in animals attributes we feel important. Sometimes they are qualities that make us feel secure; we praise the dog for his faithfulness. Sometimes they are qualities we hope we lack and which therefore make us shine by comparison; we talk of the stupidity of the cow, the gluttony of the hog, the empty-headedness of the chicken, the cowardice of the jackal. Sometimes they are qualities we secretly feel we are lacking or losing; we admire (or resent) the independence of the cat, the racoon's intelligence.

One quality I have noticed we increasingly seek in animals is that of freedom. We see a horse running across a field, and in our minds he is transformed into a wild horse racing over the steppes or the prairie. A wild elephant, if you have ever encountered one, projects an extraordinary sense of unassailable liberty. But the horse will be saddled or slaughtered for dog food, and the elephant will be killed by a poacher for ivory or rounded up and captured to walk, gold-caparisoned, in the marriage procession of an Indian prince. The only creatures whose freedom we can by and large rely on are the birds. We kill them, we cage them, but always enough remain for that free soaring which, like the thought of poets,

. . . talks of the end of cages.

And so, we love and envy them.

THE BITTERSWEET
SMELL OF FAILURE

There is something vulgar in all success; the greatest men fail, or seem to have failed.

Oscar Wilde, as quoted in
Vincent O'Sullivan, *Aspects of
Wilde*

The young writer Vincent O'Sullivan was one of the few people who befriended Oscar Wilde in those dark days after his release from prison, when he lived out his last few years in exile, impoverished and shunned by the respectable and even by some of the disreputable. When Wilde talked about success and failure, he and O'Sullivan were discussing the Irish nationalist leader Charles Stewart Parnell, who had fallen from a position of enormous influence through the kind of intrusion of personal life into public career of which we have recently seen so many examples in the United States; he was named as correspondent in a divorce case, and that brought an abrupt end to a brilliant career.

But when he said this, Wilde must also have been thinking of his own downfall. A few years earlier, his plays, the most brilliant of their age, were playing to packed houses; he was in demand in the best homes as the wittiest dinner guest London society had known in decades; he stood at the very centre of the literary culture of the 1890s, with its emphasis on decadence and dandyism. Then he was charged with homosexual acts that in our day are no longer criminal offences, was immured in one of the barbarous unreformed prisons of the Victorian age, and his career was ended, his promise destroyed, his friends lost. All he wrote afterward was that great indictment of prisons and the criminal law, *The Ballad of Reading Gaol*.

Wilde was not talking only in afterthought when he made his remark to O'Sullivan. Throughout his literary career, which has been splendidly traced in a recent biography by Richard Ellmann, one finds the preoccupation with failure. What, after all, is that strange novel, *The Picture of Dorian Gray*, but a fictional anticipation of the failure that must end a life devoted to hedonistic pursuits? Wilde was not alone in his preoccupation with failure. That very different writer, George Orwell, once remarked that every life, seen from the inside, is a failure. And so it is, in a way, for all but the shallowest monsters of self-satisfaction. We all have self-images we never live up to, and I doubt if there is a creative person who dies with the sense that he or she has completely fulfilled the promise. There is always that great undone work, that ungrasped opportunity which was needed for complete fulfilment.

But these, of course, are internalized failures that Orwell talks about. Wilde was concerned with the externalized failures which take on the dimensions of tragedy because in the full gaze of the world they show a person destroyed by the flaws of his own nature, by the pride against the gods which the Greeks called *hubris*. Wilde, of course, was an example in real life of *hubris* leading to tragic failure.

And it is revealing of our almost obsessive preoccupation as a society with the idea of failure that almost all our great works of literature and drama are concerned with it. Think of the number of great novels that in one way or another end in the failure that comes from a flawed vision of success: *Madame Bovary, Le Rouge et le Noir, Anna Karenina, Fathers and Sons, Nostromo, The Return of the Native, Don Quixote*; the list could go on indefinitely. And these are only the novels that end in death. Those that concern the lesser manifestations of failure and end in mere disillusionment are legion. And what do we consider the great plays of Shakespeare? *Hamlet, Macbeth, King Lear, Julius Caesar, Antony and Cleopatra*, all chronicles of splendid failure. Failure in various forms permeates the plays of Ibsen and Chekhov and dominates Greek tragedy. The same pattern runs in major poetry. The hero of *Paradise*

Lost is not God but that grandiose failure, Satan, and even in Dante's *Divine Comedy*, whose overt intent is to lead men towards salvation, it is the atrocious failures, those who have sinned their way into hell, who are the most fascinating.

Why do the chronicles of failure so fascinate us in literature and drama and even film? (Witness the interest aroused by Bertolucci's *The Last Emperor*.) Why do we follow almost gloatingly the latest news of a politician or a hot gospeller ruined by an amatory indiscretion, or of a fabulously rich and successful financier being taken in handcuffs from Wall Street because he overstepped the line of dishonesty accepted in the money world?

Another of Wilde's friends, Max Beerbohm, had one explanation when he let one of the characters in his novel *Zuleika Dobson* remark that "the dullard's envy of brilliant men is always assuaged by the suspicion that they will come to a bad end"; he was probably thinking of the obscene burst of joy on the part of the righteous on the day Wilde was sent to prison. But it is not merely a question of dullards envying the success of their betters, as the list of great writers who have made failure their subject demonstrates. It is something about success itself that we inherently distrust. There is an honesty about failure. The tragic failures have paid their price, and so we accept them finally to our hearts. But with the successful, as with the completely good, we always feel there is something concealed, the flaw in the dam that will one day break open, and so we reserve our approval. "Call no man happy till the day he dies . . ." said the Greek sage Solon, and I think that comes to our minds when we read stories of success. Hence the ill repute of happy endings.

But there is also the aesthetic aspect of success. Wilde was not the only writer to describe it as "vulgar"; Edmund Burke remarked that success is "the only infallible criterion of wisdom to vulgar minds." And when we look at the aesthetics of success, we realize that what makes it seem vulgar to sensitive minds is the fact that it stands always in the full light; there is no doubting shadow, and that is what makes it unnatural and inhuman. For nature and life are light-and-shadow mingled, and the lives of the great failures show precisely that, the play of light and shadow at its most dramatic. They are ourselves made larger, and so the internal failure of which Orwell talked and the external failure that Wilde exemplified come together. We not only identify in imagination with Lear and Antony, with Anna Karenina and Bazarov. In our own small, potential way, we *are* them. "Madame Bovary — c'est moi!"

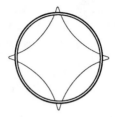

PRUFROCK'S LAMENT

I love long life better than gifts.

Shakespeare,
Anthony and Cleopatra

I grow old . . . I grow old . . .
I shall wear the bottoms of my trousers rolled.

T.S. Eliot,
The Love Song of J. Alfred Prufrock

The other day I was invited to write an essay for one of those large and earnest symposiums that American institutes sometimes gather together and publish. This time it was on growing old, and as I began to dip through some familiar quotations and fan outward from there, I realized more than ever before the variety of responses to aging that writers have shown. Yeats had a great deal to say about it, and especially about the contrast between the deteriorating shell of a person and the kernel of spirit within.

> An aged man is but a paltry thing.
> A tattered coat upon a stick, unless
> Soul clap its hands and sing, and louder sing
> For every tatter in its mortal dress.

But the two pieces I found fascinating, and especially in their contrast, were *Anthony and Cleopatra* and *The Love Song of J. Alfred Prufrock*, that extraordinary work with which in the 1920s T.S. Eliot opened up to young writers a whole vista of new poetic possibilities.

The main theme of *Anthony and Cleopatra* is the obsessive power of love; indeed, John Dryden wrote a rather good rhyming version of the play which he called *All for Love: Or, the World Well Lost*. But the secondary theme is surely the relativity of age. Talk about age and long life recurs throughout the play, often rather ironically when we think of what happens to the characters. "I love long life better than figs," jests the maid Charmian at the beginning, though she will have died young by the last scene. And almost immediately afterwards Cleopatra gives a clue to the secondary theme when she says:

> Though age from folly could not give me freedom,
> It does from childishness . . .

And the theme is perhaps best marked off by the later remark of Enobarbus, gossiping about Cleopatra:

> Age cannot wither her, nor custom stale
> Her infinite variety . . .

All these hints are meant to lead us to the astonishing fact that Cleopatra, this beauty for whom men would give their lives, this amorous dynamo, this fabled "serpent of old Nile," was not exactly a paragon of youth. She was a mature woman on the edge of forty, and Anthony was a man in his middle fifties, which in Roman and Elizabethan terms meant the verge of old age. (People in their *forties* are called old in Jane Austen's novels as late as the early nineteenth century.) Shakespeare himself, after all, at the end of a long life's work, died a year younger than Anthony. So if one wanted a good sub-title for the play, the best might well be "Old Love's Dream." Shakespeare is telling us, as Plutarch told him, that the emotions are not measured by our conventional ideas about youth and age, that it may be absurd to be old and to love, but in the absurdity perhaps lies the wonder.

And then we come to the case of T.S. Eliot, in 1917 a bank clerk of less than thirty with a taste for bawdy songs, writing a poem in which his alter ego, Prufrock, laments growing old — having lived in imagination through all the predicaments of human existence — and thinks of all the trivial preoccupations of an aimless life.

> Shall I part my hair behind? Do I dare to eat a peach?
> I shall wear white flannel trousers, and walk upon the beach.
> I have heard the mermaids singing, each to each.
>
> I do not think that they will sing to me.

One gets the impression from the accounts of his contemporaries that there was always something prematurely old and a little fusty about Eliot in his youth, and one is reminded of Wilde's remark about Max Beerbohm, that the gods had conferred on him "the gift of perpetual old age." There are those — and we all know them — who go through their younger lives pursued by the sense of responsibility supposed to be characteristic of old people, so that though they may perhaps share in the pleasures of youth, they do so without fervour, as a kind of duty, a *rite de passage* to be endured before they settle down into the comforts of seniority.

Either extreme, Anthony or Max Beerbohm as Wilde saw him, offended against the conventional wisdom expressed in the saying, "Be your age," the idea of a steady progression, mind, body, and feelings keeping in step, through what used to be called "The Seven Ages of Man." (One never hears of "The Seven Ages of Woman," which makes me suspect that this was a male, patriarchal concept, which women evaded by the traditional ruse of never telling their ages.) Max, as the perpetual oldster, would presumably escape all the penalties of juvenile folly and youthful excess, but would end up with a deficiency of accumulated experience. Anthony — well, we know how Anthony ended, forced to commit suicide through falling into the hands of the enemies who had once seemed his friends. But until that end there was the absurd glory of the aging man who defied the death he foresaw in the only way he knew — by acting as if he were young for ever. In this way he was surely one of the great existentialist heroes, defying death by living on the brink. And perhaps in the end Prufrock's creator, if not Prufrock himself, realized there was something more to growing old than a mere *taedium vitae* — a weariness with life. For Eliot, when he was an old man, loved a young woman and married her, and lived perhaps the only happy years of his life. In the end, the mermaids sang for him.

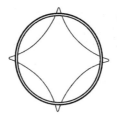

THE UNFORGIVEABLE
SIN OF IGNORANCE

Blessed ignorance! That unforgiveable sin of trans-Atlantic civilization . . . .

Veronika said, "I guess we need them both, Prague and freedom. But the way things are, we can't have both. It's either-or."

Josef Skvorecky,
The Engineer of Human Souls

If I were asked to judge a competition for the best novel published during the 1980s in Canada, I would pick Josef Skvorecky's *The Engineer of Human Souls*, not only for its fine style (splendidly rendered into English by Paul Wilson), its perceptive insights into characters, its magical use of memory, but also — and perhaps most of all — for its complex awareness of the social and political realities of our lives and times.

The Engineer is a cunningly collaged book whose action unfolds between two worlds: democratic Canada where — despite an ominous growth of puritanical interferences — we still enjoy a good deal of real freedom; and the totalitarian realms where freedoms are few and the liberty to speak and write as one wishes is perennially precarious. The sense of a divided world is increased by the fact that the book was written in Canada, but in Skvorecky's own language of Czech, though he teaches English literature at the University of Toronto. It is in some ways a classic central European novel offering the same kind of realism with a romantic overlay as appeared in Thomas Mann's novels. It fits well into the category which Germans call *Künstlerroman*, the story of an artist's development, yet it is also the portrait of a people — the Czech people — going through the repeated crises of the twentieth century.

Skvorecky is not only a master of fiction; he is also a man with a message: the liberating and subversive nature of art. This makes *The Engineer of Human Souls* unusual among recent Canadian literature, where the novel with a message went out with Hugh MacLennan. Rather, it finds its place in a kind of fiction that has long flourished in Europe east of the Atlantic and south of the English Channel, but has rarely been naturalized in the English-speaking literatures. This is the novel in which the effects of political events and systems shape the lives of the characters; its moving impetus lies in the interaction between the domineering state and the individual who seeks to resist or evade it. This kind of fiction dates far back in the nineteenth century to Turgenev (*Virgin Soil*) and Stendhal (*Le Rouge et Le Noir.*) It became particularly important during the 1930s, with totalitarian systems rising up everywhere on the European continent from Russia to Spain. Such writers as André Malraux and Ignazio Silone, Arthur Koestler and Albert Camus, made the socio-political struggle, with the rebel individual as protagonist, the central preoccupation of their novels. Only one writer in England had the same kind of political prescience at that time; he was George Orwell, who recognized the totalitarian threat in *Coming Up for Air* (1938) even before he wrote his more celebrated books, *Animal Farm* and *Nineteen Eighty Four*. And Orwell made the same accusation of "Blessed ignorance! That unforgiveable sin" against the English and their writers as Skvorecky has done against the Canadians a generation later.

For me the great virtue of books like Malraux's *La Condition humaine* and Silone's *Bread and Wine* and Orwell's novels is that they insist by implication that the heart of a piece of fiction is not its style or form, which are the skin and the skeleton of a work, but its content, the moral and intellectual core. *The Engineer of Human Souls* has this vital core of content, a vision of freedom perpetually imperilled, and a parallel collective vision of the Czech people, separated yet united, some carrying on as best they can in their own country and others living in exile among bewildering Canadians. It is not only a remarkable political novel, but also a fascinating social study of the way cultures and traditions change yet continue in exile. As a final bonus, it is at times an extremely funny book, in a way resembling that famous and masterly account of rebellion by evasion, *The Good Soldier Schweik*, by now a Czech classic.

If fate ever puts Canadians in the situation where politics impinges hostilely on our lives, the situation where artists are called to make their work a Marathon in defence of freedom, *The Engineer of Human Souls* will be an inspiration for our writers. As a novel of political awareness and responsibility, it has no rival in Canadian literature, which was greatly enriched by Josef Skvorecky's arrival two decades ago. Skvorecky brought to us more than a major literary talent, more than the important emigré Czech-language publishing house he and his wife founded. He brought a challenge to look with clear eyes at the world around us, so that we can understand why people flee to Canada in search of freedom, but also so that we can be alert to the dangers that may one day threaten our own freedoms.

As the Irish patriot John Philpot Curran put it long ago, at the end of the eighteenth century: "The condition upon which God hath given liberty to man is eternal vigilance."

WILD OATS IN
THE RAIN FOREST

*In fact, the hotel was doing good business that night. The whirlpool,
as a temperance tract might say, was a-booming and a-boiling,
sucking down men's wages and perhaps their health. The boys were
"on the tear," and the hotel resounded with their revelry . . . the
scene reminded me a little of boating suppers and undergraduates;
but the action, of course, was much more vigorous, as befitted
grown-up men.*

M. Allerdale Grainger,
Woodsmen of the West

Woodsmen of the West is surely the most curious of Canadian classics,
and it must have made strange reading in many a Canadian household
when it was published in 1908 at the height of the great temperance
campaigns. For if there was ever an uninhibited account of the areas of
Canadian society where the temperance movement and all its works
were vehemently rejected, it was this dense and darkly comic little
novel about the life of the itinerant forest workers in western Canada
during the years before the Great War. For me it has a special, personal
kind of interest, because — though in a much less lurid way — my own
experience on the West Coast in the 1950s touched the same territory
as Grainger's half a century before, and I knew some of the last survi-
vors of the generation of wild "bush apes" he described.

Grainger was in fact a rather unlikely kind of man to become involved with the rough, barely educated drifters who manned the forest camps at the turn of the century, taking as much punishment in their recreation as they did in the hard conditions of the lumber camps at this period. He was a young Englishman of good family who went to King's College, Cambridge, and then in 1897 was caught up in the lure of the Klondike. He placer-mined unsuccessfully. He worked on the river boats of the Yukon. He fought in the South African War, and then he returned to Canada and for a time became a working logger.

It is this period of deep immersion in the hard and roisterous life of the coast that he embodied in *Woodsmen of the West*, which is really a chunk of fictionalized autobiography telling with little disguise his experiences working in the remote camps at the heads of far inlets where the rain forest came down to salt water, and taking part, mainly as the observant spectator, in the wild goings-on in the rough hotels scattered along the coast. Much of the book is so true to life that the local British Columbian publisher Howie White, who runs a magazine of regional history called *Raincoast Chronicles* from one of the coastal inlets near where Grainger worked, has been able to trace the originals of most of the hotels that feature so wildly in the novel.

What makes Grainger so interesting as a person is the way his life was divided up. Not long ago I was talking to an old friend (old in the sense of long-term and, also, in the sense of being, as she would put it, "somewhat more antique" than I) who had moved in the highly English-oriented society of Victoria in the years between the great wars. She talked at length about the people she had known and happened to mention Allerdale Grainger. Immediately I talked of *Woodsmen of the West*, and she showed equally immediate astonishment that the man she had known, as head of the British Columbian forestry service, should have strayed so far from the province of a high Victoria bureaucrat as to write a book of any kind, let alone a novel. When I took down *Woodsmen* and read some selected passages (even more roisterous than the one I have just quoted) she was, to all appearance, flabbergasted. Clearly Grainger, who after all came from the right background and the right family, straight out of the English top drawer, had been able to slip back into respectability after his wild life, and to adopt the protective colouring of a dignified civil servant living in a fine Tudor style house in a select area of Victoria.

But perhaps the hint of continuity was there, even in *Woodsmen*, with its comparison between drunken loggers and "boating suppers and undergraduates." Grainger was a student who carried the zest of boating suppers and undergraduate pranks into the world of adventure — Klondike or South Africa — and into the different pranks of "grown-up" men, before he returned by a circuitous route to the responsible life of a loyal official and a good citizen. He was not the only young public school Brit to follow this pattern on the West Coast. The writer Roderick Haig-Brown was another who served his apprenticeship in the woods of the Pacific North West. Later Rod became not only a famous writer, but in many other ways, like Grainger, a pillar of society, magistrate and university chancellor. Yet whenever I cross the border and go down through the rough little American town of Sedro-Wooley, I remember it was here that as a young stripling Haig-Brown made much of his living as a prize fighter; a good training in boxing at Charterhouse enabled him to deliver expert knockouts to lumber camp roustabouts almost twice his weight. He was a kind of slim David among gorilla Goliaths.

"Sowing your wild oats" they called it in those days, and one of the great advantages of the far-flung Empire on which the sun never set was that it provided so many fields where the sowing could take place, and plenty of opportunity to grow the good crop of a career after the wild grain had been reaped. I wonder where such young English men sow their wild oats now.

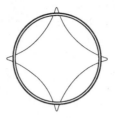

LITTLE MAGAZINES AND
THE IRONIES OF FATE

*I am informally connected with a couple of new and impecunious
papers . . . the latter can pay a little, the former practically cannot
pay at all, we do it for larks.*

> Ezra Pound to James Joyce,
> December 13, as quoted by
> Julian Symons, *Makers of the New:
> The Revolution in Literature 1912–1939*

I am sure what Pound said to Joyce in 1913, when both were young
writers on whom fame (or — in Pound's case — notoriety) had not yet
descended, must have been said a thousand times, in very much the
same words, by other young writers to each other over the generations.
What they stress is the extraordinarily role that small, precariously
funded magazines read by at most a few hundred people have played in
the development of literature during the present century.

Pound was an enthusiastic promoter of such magazines, for which he
also wrote profusely. I suspect the two magazines he meant when he
wrote to Joyce were *Poetry (Chicago)*, which Harriet Monroe founded
at the end of 1912, and *The Egoist*, whose first number appeared early
in 1914, largely through Pound's efforts. *Poetry (Chicago)* has
miraculously survived for more than three quarters of a century under
a succession of talented editors, but *The Egoist* did not last long, and
the same applies to yet another magazine founded in 1914, also with
the busy help of Pound, *The Little Review*.

The Little Review, which Margaret Anderson edited with various associates from 1914 to 1929, was probably the best and certainly the most celebrated of all the Modernist magazines, and though it lived up to its name in size and circulation and carried on a chancy existence, it published the new writers who would dominate the next decades in anglophone literature; not only Pound, but also T.S. Eliot, Hart Crane, Ernest Hemingway, and James Joyce, the first parts of whose masterpiece, *Ulysses*, found publication in its pages. *The Little Review* became the prototype of the *avant garde* literary journal, and to this day, in memory of it, we still call such efforts "little magazines," no matter what their size.

Ever since that time, and in almost every country, the little magazine — read by a few people, seeking out new talents, offering them exposure rather than cash — has been one of the symptoms of a healthy and growing literature. In the development of Canadian literature, for example, the little magazines played a central and essential role. The *McGill Fortnightly Review*, in the hands of F.R. Scott and A.J.M. Smith during the late 1920s, signalled the beginning of a real Modern Movement in Canadian poetry. Other little magazines in the 1940s, like *Preview* and *First Statement*, with which Irving Layton and Raymond Souster and P.K. Page were connected, sustained the impetus, which was later carried on by *Northern Review*, edited by John Sutherland, Donald's brother. In these magazines most of the first generation of modern Canadian poets began their careers. What new geniuses are emerging in the little magazines of the 1980s only time will reveal, but I would suggest that subscribing to such journals is a sound cultural investment even if in the short run a doubtful financial one. Though I suspect anyone who invested in the *Little Review* in 1914 and sold his copies today would make a handsome profit in the rare book market.

What happens to the writers who are discovered by little magazines is part of the same grotesque lottery of acceptance by posterity whose extremity was shown when tens of millions of dollars were paid recently for paintings Vincent Van Gogh had made when he was on the verge of starvation for lack of patrons. In *Makers of the New*, the excellent work of literary history from which I picked the quotation that begins this essay, Julian Symons (himself the editor of an influential little magazine of the late 1930s, *Twentieth Century Verse*), shows how the great modernist writers, Pound and Eliot, Joyce and Wyndham Lewis, working through little magazines and daring experimental publishers, changed the whole character of literature in their age. But their personal fates, even when fame reached them, varied considerably. Pound's fame turned into notoriety, when he supported the fascists during World War II, and he remains a centre of controversy. Wyndham Lewis, craggy and uncompromising, never gained the recognition his talents as both a painter and a writer deserved. Joyce became a financial success only after his death, and then because his works were taken up by the academic critics he despised and sold widely as university texts.

But the most curious of all these fates is that of the staid T.S. Eliot, the rhapsode of social decay in *The Waste Land*, the philosophic poet of modern High Anglicanism in *Four Quartets*, for his fame has suddenly and posthumously blossomed because of a work he did as a mild joke. Pound's nickname for Eliot was "Old Possum," and one day in a moment of demure fun Eliot wrote *Old Possum's Book of Practical Cats*, which is not even mentioned in serious articles about his poetry. Yet, transmuted into the musical review *Cats*, it has swept the English-speaking world, introduced some of Eliot's lightest verse to millions, and made a pretty posthumous penny. Perhaps the happiest result, of which I heard only the other day, is that with the million pounds or so that was its share of the sale of rights on *Old Possum's Book*, the fine British publishing firm of Faber & Faber, of which old Possum was so long a director, had been able to fight off takeover bids and maintain its independence, continuing to publish the poets who make their debuts in little magazines. For once, the caprice of the Gods has led to a fitting end.

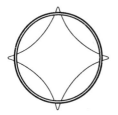

THE GEM-LIKE FLAME OF ART

The service of philosophy, and of . . . culture as well, to the human spirit, is to startle it into a sharp and eager observation. Not the fruit of experience, but experience itself is the end . . . . To burn always with this hard gem-like flame, to maintain this ecstacy, is success in life.

Walter Pater,
The Renaissance

Walter Pater was perhaps the strongest of all rebels against Victorian orthodoxy: a timid Oxford don living soberly with his spinster sisters and so shy that his lectures were mumbled, and on one occasion, when he anxiously asked some of his friends if they had heard what he said, Oscar Wilde answered: "We overheard you, dear Walter." Yet, almost unwillingly, Pater became one of the standard bearers for the intellectual and artistic rebellion of the late Victorian age.

Pater was a passionate aesthete, devoted to detecting the perfect form, to fostering the perfect mood, and when he wrote his famous book *The Renaissance* in 1873, he gave expression to thoughts that could only appear blasphemous to respectable Victorian Christians. His studies of artists in the past and the reasons for the appeal of their work led him to see the role of art as giving a "quickened sense of life"; it was the only way of reconciling "the splendour of existence and its awful brevity."

By laying the stress on experience itself, on the value of the moment, Pater was denying the Victorian view of life as a mere path towards the splendid destination of Heaven or the appalling destination of Hell. Life now, not later, was what mattered to Pater, and he summed up his attitude in a passionate plea for another wisdom than that of conventional religion:

> Of this wisdom, the poetic passion, the desire for beauty, and love of art for art's sake has most; for art comes to you professing frankly to give nothing but the highest quality to your moments as they pass, and simply for those moments' sake.

Not only did Pater promote a view of art for art's sake, rather than art in the service of religion or politics or morality, he also gave a new definition to "success in life." It was no longer a matter of laying up treasure either on earth or in heaven. It was a matter of burning always with "this hard gem-like flame" of perpetually alert perception, aesthetic ecstacy.

Well may the Victorians — to Pater's alarm — have been outraged by such a conclusion, for Pater was in fact reiterating the view of the pagans of ancient Greece and Rome, who set little store on the world beyond death, which they regarded as a wretched state where the ghosts of the dead wandered in the twilit afterlife of Hades, and who stressed the glory of immediate earthly existence. The Roman poet Horace put it in a famous line, *carpe diem, quam minimum credula postero*, which means, roughly, "enjoy today, since you can never be sure of tomorrow"; or, as the seventeenth-century English poet Robert Herrick later said, in a more familiar poem, archly entitled, "To Virgins, to Make Much of Time":

> Gather ye rosebuds while ye may,
> Old Time is still a-flying:
> And this same flower that smiles today,
> To-morrow will be dying.

If Pater shocked the orthodox, who interpreted his remarks as giving licence to uninhibited behaviour, the young writers and artists of the time hailed him as a liberator. Oscar Wilde called *The Renaissance* his "Golden Book." And as the young men of the Nineties, the self-styled Decadents, made a cult of immediate sensation, and experimented with drink and drugs and unconventional sexuality, all of which had a glamour of Forbidden Sin they have largely lost in our permissive times, the mumbling Fellow of Brasenose College became their not entirely willing prophet. He was not the first writer to be shocked when his words became the inspiration of action.

Pater has been dead now almost a hundred years (he died in 1894) and the young hedonists of the 1890s are mostly as forgotten as Herrick's fading rosebuds, yet all these decades afterwards Pater's phrase, "to burn always with this hard gem-like flame," still haunts the mind, perhaps because over the years its meaning has subtly changed.

A few years ago I wrote a long letter of affection and sympathy to a good friend of mine, a writer I thought was dying of cancer. And she replied: "I shall go on burning with my hard, gem-like flame"; to everyone's astonishment her flame is still burning, bright and clear as a jewel, in the remission she virtually willed for herself. And this I feel offers a good example of the way phrases can change their meaning as times and contexts alter.

Our society is less attached to the so-called eternal verities and more inclined to accept experience for its immediate sake than the Victorians. It needs no Paterian exhortations to this effect. And in these circumstances the symbol of the "hard, gem-like flame," which combines the rigidity of a jewel with the fluency of a flame, shifts its connotation and becomes a sign of consistency. I use it myself as a kind of motto, and what it suggests to me is not the search for momentary sensation, but the artist's dedication to the creative life, to the process by which out of the flame of making comes the hard jewel of the work which remains when the maker's fire has been extinguished. The phrase has come to mean the strength of lasting impulses rather than the intensity of momentary impressions. Like a work of art, in other words, Pater's famous saying has taken on a life of its own, a bright and enduring austerity, beyond its creator's life and beyond his intent.

AND I QUOTE

A book that furnishes no quotations is, me judice, *no book — it is a plaything.*

Thomas Love Peacock,
Crotchet Castle

Quotations are, so to speak, the lifeblood of these little essays I have been writing, but this is the first time I have begun with a quotation about quotations. Thomas Love Peacock was, of course, a master of the quotable book. He wrote a series of brilliant conversational novels — *Headlong Hall* and *Nightmare Abbey* are even better known and cleverer than *Crotchet Castle* — in which characters who are thinly disguised versions of well-known contemporaries (Byron and Coleridge, Godwin and Shelley) seek to shine in comparison with each other and so fire off an endless series of opinions shaped in epigrammatic form. Peacock's great disciple was Aldous Huxley, who, in novels like *Crome Yellow* and *Antic Hay*, merely transferred Peacock's method into the twentieth century and presented his own series of quotable characters based on contemporaries like Bertrand Russell and Lytton Strachey, Nancy Cunard and Lady Ottoline Morell.

I have been prompted to this celebration of the quotation by the newest publication of John Robert Colombo, the Grand Magpie of Canadian Letters. As gatherer of facts about Canada, he is without a rival, and his good-humored reference books, like *Colombo's Canadian References* and *Colombo's Book of Canada*, are volumes many writers consult without admitting it. His *Canadian Literary Landmarks*, which appeared a few years ago, is an entertaining geography of literary Canada, linking up writers and the places associated with them, and in the process illustrating how important place and space are in our culture. But Colombo's series of aphoristic dictionaries — *Colombo's Canadian Quotations, Colombo's Concise Canadian Quotations,* and the recently published *Colombo's New Canadian Quotations* — are undoubtedly the books for which we owe him the greatest debt, and by which he is likely to be longest remembered. The *New Canadian Quotations* expands his range enormously: out of 4600 entries — the fruit of a prodigious industry in collecting and selecting — 4000 are new in the sense of not having been Colombized before.

One is tempted to compare Colombo's collections of quotations with the great British dictionaries of this kind, like the Oxford and the Penguin, but I think there is a real difference in content that points to essential divergences between Canadian and British cultural attitudes. The British dictionaries are still really imperial works, gathering up, like the museums of conquerors, the wealth of wit and wisdom from all ages and all lands. Colombo's dictionaries are by implication nationalist. They take the heritage of the ages and the continents for granted, and offer us nothing but homegrown wisdom.

All of which tends to concentrate the mind. What we see, preserved in one- or two- or three-liners, and, at most, in ten-liners, is the fragmented yet accumulated wisdom of a people considering itself and its relation to the world, to the petty affairs of mundane Canadian existence as well as to the grand questions of life. We hear unexpected things like René Lévesque's view of monarchy: "Better we have the Queen as Head of State than, say, Keith Davey"; and Margaret Atwood's quiet cynicism about love: "The desire to be loved is the last illusion: Give it up and you will be free." Louis Dudek is outrageous on Canadian literature: "Canadian literature is very interesting so long as you don't bother to read it." And Arthur Porter, Chairman of the Royal Commission on Electric Power Planning, is even more outrageous on nuclear waste: "If King Tut's tomb could have been stored 4000 years without being disrupted, then we can certainly store nuclear waste."

Naturally, as a constant user of quotations, I was pleased, though at times a little disturbed, to find myself quoted no less than 17 times in the *New Canadian Quotations.* I applauded myself gently for saying, a decade ago, in *The Times Literary Supplement*, "Often one feels that if a true federalism survives anywhere in Canada, it does among the artists with their intense local loyalties and their countrywide links," and I applauded Colombo for tracing so remote a source. I also felt I had expressed an insight which historians will bear out when I said, in 1979: "I regard Pierre Trudeau as perhaps the leading enemy of a workable Canadian unity, and René Lévesque as perhaps its greatest friend, since he has awakened us to the perils of an artificial constitutional unity that will not take into account the various needs and aspirations of the regions." Still, it is always a little uncanny to find one's words floating back to one like echoes disembodied because they have lost their context, and doubly so when it is an echo of an echo, as in my attempt to define a Canadian: "I confess that on one occasion of bewilderment, of which I am reminded every time I look into *Colombo's Canadian Quotations*, the only foolproof definition of a Canadian that occurred to me was that he was a North American who does not owe allegiance to the United States or Mexico."

Yet, as the echoes lie down, I find myself just as addicted as ever to quotations, those nuggets from the great mother lode of human wisdom that can encapsulate the whole spirit of a book, the whole direction of a poet's thought. Like Peacock, I like my books to be quotable.